Diego's Brooklyn

by Adrian Del Valle

This is a work of fiction. Any resemblance in this novel to anyone's character, alive or dead, including those based on real people or events or locales, is entirely coincidental and are products of the author's imagination or are used fictitiously and meant as entertainment only.
Copyright © 2015 Adrian Del Valle
All rights reserved.

ISBN: 1482040468
ISBN 13: 9781482040463

Other novels by Adrian DelValle

Yesterday in the Cavern's Dark;

Of fire spirits and men

Curby

Searching for the Sun

Dedication

For my sister, Lucy and brother Valentine

Table of contents

Dedication v

Dean Street 1

Making Money 9

Friends 25

P.S. 6 45

Hell's Kitchen 55

The Steel Box 97

Loose Ends and Loan Sharks 125

Epilogue 157

Chapter One
Dean Street

Welcome to my stoop. I lived in this three story building behind me too many years to disclose the actual number to you, because that would give away my age. Yeah, I'm an old guy, born and raised right here in downtown Brooklyn, but this story isn't about me. It's about a young boy of fourteen who lived with his mom right down the street. He was a nice kid, and his mom, too, both the nicest people that ever turned a pair of well-worn converse sneakers and beat up dress shoes into the old brownstone at 240 Dean Street.

You wouldn't think that a pleasant block like this, with tree lined maples and clean sidewalks, could hold a most amazing story as the one I'm about to tell you. So take a seat on these steps, relax and give this old fool your undivided attention. You won't be disappointed, I promise you.

The 200 block of Dean Street, in 1961, was typical of Boerum Hill, a mixed neighborhood near the Manhattan and Brooklyn Bridges. Brownstone row-houses lined both sides of the street from corner to corner. Fat wrought iron gates, thick with layers of black paint, enclosed front patches of dirt ten feet square.

The heyday of once proud, manicured gardens were replaced with the ignored nuisances of unintended growth—a place to put tin garbage cans and worn out bicycles. Oh, sure, the occasional well-kept frontage was also there, along with an occasional magnolia or cherry tree. A few caring souls even found a bit of free time in their hectic schedules to plant a tulip or two, but most were overgrown with weeds or cemented in.

This is a land formed by glaciers that gouged out valleys and carried boulders the size of houses down from Canada. Before that, hadrosaurs ran from the likes of a cousin of T-Rex. Let's just call him chompasourus, for now. I don't have time to hoof it all the way to the library to find out, okay? So, let's get on with the story.

It's hard to imagine that only 350 years ago this was a pristine wilderness inhabited by Indian tribes like the Carnarsie in Brooklyn and the Manhattans on the other side of the East River. Both belonged to the greater Delaware language group that today would have populated lands from Nassau County to Eastern Pennsylvania and south to as far as the state of Delaware.

Hard also, to picture woods teeming with deer, beaver and bear. Marshes bordered these shores and in the spring offered migrating ducks for the cooking pot. Blue claw crabs moved north to breed in these bountiful waters, with clams and striped bass plentiful as well. And from these marshes also came clouds of mosquitoes, the only relief for the Indians, a generous helping of rancid bear grease spread over the entire body.

Then came the Dutch in the 1600's, followed by the English, the French and black slaves. Plots of land a block wide and five or so blocks long were allotted to those who would farm it. A few of their names still grace some of the street signs to this day.

Elms and maples now line both sides of Dean Street, their canopies mushrooming above the height of the roofs. And there are lots of cats, strays of a variety of colors and patterns. They forage inside garbage cans, and patrol up and down the block and through vacant lots for rats.

Most landlords take up residences on the first floors and sometimes first two. The unfortunates live upstairs, renting one or two room flats. None of the tenants have private bathrooms. Those are shared one to a floor with all of the rooms facing common hallways. Single men usually occupy the small 9x12's on the top floors. Many of the larger furnished units on the first are grabbed up by the Department of Welfare to house single mothers and the unemployable.

This was fourteen year old Diego Rivera's Brooklyn, a land of wealth as well as a land of have-nots. And for those poorer unfortunates, it is fully roach infested and bare of extras.

It's summer and it's hot, hot like cheap, dime store plastic curtains blowing out of wide open windows, hot. Air conditioning is unheard of. The ancient wiring would have none of it. Instead, rickety old fans spin noisily on table tops and next to bed sides.

The worst of the poor lone minions reside on the top floors beneath dark tar roofs that absorb the heat of the sun the entire day. When it's 90 outside, the top floors can reach temperatures of 100 or more. Add to that the New York City humidity that can climb above 90 percent, and you learn the real meaning of sweating in your sheets. The only relief is ice in a rag, but these are upper furnished rooms, remember? No kitchen, no fridge---no fridge, no ice.

A bucket of tap water is all you have for the night, something to dip a rag into when you wake from that dripping sweat in the middle of pitch blackness. That is, if the rats haven't either sucked up the last of it, or drowned in the bucket trying.

Three buildings in from the corner of Nevins, 240 Dean Street sits unobtrusively among a row of indistinguishable brownstones. Room 2B, is the 9x12 home of Joe Barnes, a forty plus loser, who's new and barely month old career is as an usher at the Fox Movie Theatre, Downtown. The job pays $1.15 an hour, minimum wage, for a five day work week from Wednesdays through Sundays. Joe's room rent is 48 baby clams a month. A couple of slices of pizza at 15 cents each takes care of most dinners. Breakfast before work is usually an egg on a roll with coffee---25 cents.

By walking the twenty blocks to work instead of taking a bus, Joe saves 15 cents. That's 30 for the round trip, or two slices of pizza, or about 20 minutes of chasing kids up and down the aisles.

Joe missed his old Irish neighborhood in Manhattan—"Hell's Kitchen". He had arrived there ten years prior by way of Hicksville, Long Island and is the reason for his lack of a city accent. He could never go back, though, not to the Kitchen, that is. He owes too much money to the Irish Mob and the old cronies are after him. Here at least the rent is cheap and who would think of looking for him in Brooklyn?

With old friends like Mickey Spillane, (no, not the WWII pilot—slash—author) who needs enemies? An upstart from the old neighborhood when he was an apprentice of Hugh Mulligan, Spillane now owns the Kitchen and is nobody to mess with.

That's who Joe owes money to, lots of money---loan shark money. At 60%, the interest on the original loan has added up pretty quickly. It was the Trotters at the race track that got him into this mess in the first place. Even with all of the wheelin' and dealin' that he was into back in the city, he didn't have the hope of catching up for a hundred years. Yeah, and Joe's idea of a pleasure cruise wasn't exactly lying crunched down in a fetal position inside of a barrel floating down the East River at high tide; or any tide for that matter. Besides, just think of all the tourist sights he would miss with his head facing those wooden planks at the bottom of that barrel. Nah! He was safe where he was. And nobody figured him to be right across the river—Philly perhaps, or way out in Vegas with the rest of the mafia wannabees.

He had the perfect job, too, hiding all day in a dark movie theatre.

The room at the back end of the hall is empty and ready for a new tenant, and has been that way for the past two months.

Mary, a middle aged, and not to be disrespectful, but she's rather rotund and the type Joe would have nothing to do with. She's rented out the front room, 2A, ever since her twenties, fifteen or so years ago.

Now, this is a room of stately size, 15X18, with a gas fireplace that doesn't work---never worked. It speaks of an era when the building was once luxurious and high-end for its time, the late 1800's. Back then, it was designed as a one family home with the children and nanny/maid taking up these very same top floor rooms.

Mary rarely challenges the stairs anymore. If she needs anything she simply calls out to a passerby in the street two floors below from her munificently, oversized window arched in stained glass. A couple of bucks are wrapped in paper and tossed out of the window with a list attached; milk, eggs, bread---and don't forget the Twinkies. And if they run out of those, she'll settle for three or four packages of Scooter Pies, or even those round, strawberry Sno-balls. Just don't come back empty handed. She's been salivating the whole time you've been gone for whatever she needs, or shouldn't need for that matter. For a buffalo nickel the local kids comply.

Entering the house from the first floor, physically the second after climbing 12 steps to the top of the front stoop, the first of two entry doors are never locked. The beveled glass is cracked and the framing is in desperate need of paint; neglected like the rest of the house. The lock works, but no one seems to have a key.

The second, inside door, strains against the hinges. Caked with more than forty layers of paint, the screws still hold well, but to a frame that no longer binds properly to the wall. The leading edge of the door scrapes along the floor and has to be pushed hard to open. The lock on this door works fine as well, but no one bothers. It's too much trouble to close, so it stays ajar even in winter.

Pass through the entryway and you come to Diego's maroon door on the left, 1A, the paint, (alligatored) and chipped. It leads to two rooms, a real luxury among the serfs; indentured servants to his lordship who resides in a sub-basement castle keep one floor below. He's a withered old fart and single all his life and has hoarded all of his precious shillings. He's got lots of those now, but little of anything else, and no family. He hates dogs and barely tolerates kids. He hates when you're late with the rent, too.

Behind Diego's front two rooms, at the back of the building, Karen and her two bratty kids luxuriate in a two room flat as well. Though they're not allowed the use of the back yard, their two expansive windows, at least six feet high, offer sweeping views of the landlord's garden of tomatoes, string beans and a grapevine that stretches the full length of the back fence. Rumor has it that an old lover was chopped up and is buried back there under the tomatoes, but that rumor belongs mostly to the kids.

Summers could be boring at times, for Diego. His best friend, Hector, was away at summer camp---luck of the draw. Other kids of well to do parents went on vacation or travelled weekends to bungalows out on Long Island, Upstate or to the Jersey Shore.

Diego occupied most of the morning watching Farmer Grey cartoons, silent reruns tolerated from the forties that cost the local network next to nothing to run. Most of the time spent watching the nine inch screen was used up adjusting the rabbit ears topped with scraps of aluminum foil for a better signal. The horizontal lines kept rolling up and down the tube and always during the best parts, never during the commercials.

He'd been out on the front stoop now for the last twenty minutes beheading flies while waiting for the garbage truck. He imagined himself a medieval knight, resplendent in armored wares, sword in hand to slay the red-eyed dragons.

"Diego, the garbage truck, I hear it coming. Make sure you bring the cans back."

"Mom...I know, I know. Go inside, you're hanging out all over the place."

"This is my house dress. I'm not showing nothing."

"Mom...please?"

"Yes...okay, okay!"

VROOM

Down the block, a white behemoth lethargically crawled its way up the street. Diego's block is lucky. The garbage men don't get to his block until after 10:30 A.M. That's a lot better than having all of that banging wake you up at 6:30, the beginning of their shift.

Bam...Crash

The men toss the cans onto the sidewalk with careless abandon. If they land right side up then fine, if not, then they're the casualties of the day and the garbage men could care less.

"Ay, Petey! Look who it is. Wassup, Diego?"

"Nothin', Louie!"

"Yo Petey, ya sees little Diego over there?"

"Yeah, I see him," said Petey, sitting in the driver's seat and smoking what was left of a well chewed cigar. "Hey Diego, how's your mudda?"

"Hi Petey, she's good. Did you find anything today?"

"Yeah…we gotcha dis pinky."

From inside the cab, the driver threw a crisp, new looking Spalding at Diego. The pink rubber ball, made by the Spalding Company, was great for handball or playing stick ball in the street.

"You want this pimple ball?" Petey held up a dirty white ball covered with bumps for the boy to see.

"Sure, Petey, thanks!"

"Agh, don't mention it. By da way…where **is** your mudda?"

"Inside! She can't come out right now."

"Naw, I wasn't sayin' nuttin' bout dat, just hello or sump'n'"

"Ayyy…Fat Tony! What are ya sleepin' inside the can?"

"Leave me alone, Petey, I'm checkin' somethin' out."

Louie, Fat Tony's loading partner, stepped out from behind the hopper and approached the next stop, 240 Dean Street, Diego's house. He took his greasy work glove off and put an arm around the boy's shoulders. "Some partner I got, huh? You see that slouch what's over there?"

Diego Nodded.

"He's gotta go through ev-very freagin' bag he sees like he's lookin' for gold. That's why we never get finished on time. Ain't that right, Petey?"

Ignoring him, Petey's focus remained on an old copy of *Playboy's* center fold of the month for December, 1955, lying salaciously across the steering wheel---Joyce Nizzari---sweet.

"Come on, move it up, Petey," Louie shouted. "That's another slouch what sits up there in the driver's seat like king poop in the butt, right Diego?"

VROOM!

"And when you get to Diego's cans, don't bang'm, Fat Tony." Louie turned to Diego again. "I guess we told him, huh, kid?"

"Can I dump a few?" The boy asked.

"Yeah, sure, go ahead. Help yourself. So…ah, what are ya gonna be, a garbage man someday?"

"Maybe?"

BAM…BANG

"Ay-y-y! You handle that pretty good, kiddo. Like a real pro. Don't he, Fat Tony? Oh, come on Tony, will ya? Get your fat head out of those smelly bags and do some work. Hey Diego, tell ol' chubby over here what I said, 'cause I'm ready to give 'm a swift kick in the ass."

Petey stuck his head out of the window of the cab and shouted above the truck noise. "Let's go! Lunch time! See ya Diego. Say hello to Ana for me."

"I'll tell her. See you on Wednesday."

Strange, how roaches know where they live. Tap the bottom of a can on the sidewalk and they fall from the bent rim underneath and scurry toward the building they came from, never to the house next door, but always to their very own Casa Grande.

With the cans returned to the building line, Diego placed all of the covers on them. He swept the front of the building and closed the outside gate. The pay wasn't much, but it was something. A week's wages covered a few pounds of rice, a can of beans, and maybe the luxury of a loaf of Italian bread once in a while.

Chapter Two
Making Money

Ana Rivera stood over the stove where she added onions to the day's soup. She was real pretty once, still is when she covers her dark, tired eyes with make-up. She had bedroom eyes, her husband used to say. Handicapped with a bad hip, she walked with a limp. On days when the pain was too much to bare, the limp became harder to conceal.

"What are you doing today? She asked, in a noticeable Spanish accent."

"I don't know," said Diego. "No one's around. Maybe I'll go downtown and make some money."

"If you make enough, pick up some milk for the cereal."

"Yeah, okay, Mom. Petey said hello by the way. He gave me this new pinky."

"Oh, si? That's nice."

"I think he likes you, Mom."

"Mm, hm."

"I don't think he's right for you, though. Besides, he's always smoking those stinky cigars."

Ana didn't answer.

Rummaging through a shoe box by the side of the couch, Diego took out a heavy Master lock with string attached and a stick of Bazooka Gum. When he got downtown to his favorite money spot in front of the Fox Theatre, he stood at his usual place at a bus stop above an iron grating covering a subway vent. Two stories below, the Lexington Avenue line rumbled by like a muffled freight train. Hot air rushed up into his face, and within the dampness, an aged stench of urine.

He unfolded a two inch Bazooka Joe comic strip that comes with a flat piece of gum. The main character wore his baseball cap sideways and had a black patch over his left eye; or was it the right eye? Diego read it a couple of times while chewing the pink gum until it was good and sticky. He then pressed it onto the bottom of the padlock and carefully lowered it with a string through the grating. He aimed toward a subway token lying on a narrow ledge 12 feet below. The token shined like new, the brass glistening like gold with the letter "Y" stamped out of it.

    Gold doubloons, Spanish coins from the 1400's; a treasure trove worth millions was below the deck of Diego's imagined Spanish Galleon. Through the heavy iron grating he could see piles of it worth millions and he would have it all.

    This was his lucky spot, the bus stop at Nevins and Flatbush. He had only cleaned it out a week ago and here he could see at least three tokens, a couple of quarters and a dime. The tokens, he could redeem for 15 cents each; a whole buck and a nickel were down there---a good day. It was enough to buy a quart of milk, a candy bar for both him and his mom and a movie ticket at the Lido. For twenty five cents, the cheap theatre on Court Street played ten cartoons, "The Three Stooges", and two feature films.

    He left for home and fifteen minutes later turned into his block on Dean Street where he saw Karen's two girls playing skully. To most of its residents, the street wasn't all gloom and doom. To Diego it was all that was familiar. It was home.

    "How much did you get?" asked Ana.

    "A dollar five."

    "You forgot to pick up the milk?"

    "I'll go in a minute, I have to use the bathroom first."

    D'avino's Grocery sat on the adjacent corner, a store owned by an old Italian couple. Holdovers from the neighborhood's better days, the D'avino's carried on like always, despite their advanced age. They were friendly to everyone even though they lived through the trials of two world wars and escaped the takeover of their country at the hands of Mussolini and the Nazi's.

    They used to sell a lot of sausages and cheese, hung from the ceiling in rows. Back then, Olives and pickles came right out of wooden barrels, as well as a dozen forms of pasta. These days, loose rice and various kinds of beans sell by the pound. Plantains and a root called yucca are prominently displayed below ripe bananas, apples and oranges. Puerto Rican spices and the cheaper cuts of meat, chicken and salted cod, sell well. Unpackaged coconut macaroons on wax paper lay on the counter by the register. Guava, mango, and coconut juice in single serve cans are popular with the newer residents.

Outside, The Daily News and New York Times sit at the forefront. To the right are the Mirror and Post, the latter two, sheepishly displaying copied headlines with steel paper weights stamped with The Daily News logo. Below, are the Spanish newspapers, la Prenza and el Diario.

Inside, fly paper hangs from the ceiling with nearly every square inch black with bug eyed carcasses. Lying on a towel at the end of the counter, a fat cat sleeps the afternoon away. In a back room, parakeets, Luciano and Annabella, chirp from the front kitchen of a rear apartment where the D'avino's live.

Diego pet the cat while waiting for the line at the counter to shorten. He finally took a spot behind the last customer, a quart of milk under his arm.

"Ay a Dieg, Howsa you motha?"

"Oh…uh, fine, Mrs. D'avino. Here's for the milk."

"Howsa you lika theesa summa. You havena gooda time? No more of the school, ay?"

"No…we finished school a month ago, already."

"A whola month? My, howza the times she's a flies, no? Here eeza you change."

"Thanks Mrs. D'avino. I gotta go, bye."

As Diego exited the store, the owner called after him. "Hey, taka care of you self. Sayza hello to Ana for me?"

Outside, ol' Bill finished up sweeping the front of the store. At six foot four, the robustly built black man from the Deep South never lost any of his muscular tone despite an advanced age of 75 plus. His hard lined, craggy face told of a difficult life of laborious jobs. There were many of those and none of them paid much. Like a lot of his generation, children had to leave school to help provide for their families. School was a luxury and poverties grip hard to break away from. It was a vicious cycle. No food on the table meant everyone had to avail themselves for work. Back in the south, children labored in coal mines, sweat shops or out in the fields for very little, and whatever they made went to the household. Without a solid education, the cycle carried on from generation to generation.

All Bill and the missus had these days to show for it was a furnished room in a basement and a paltry social security check to live on. Surplus government food, dispensed once a month, helped; a block of American cheese, a can of peanut butter, a brick of butter, 1 five pound bag of rice and a 2 pound box of corn meal.

Their furnished room is in a three story brick over on Bergen Street, one block away. They were lucky. It's an absentee landlord building and only three steps down from street level. They have a worn sink, an old noisy fridge, a stove with two burners and a large bed in the corner of the room. Bill even had the use of the yard, though it had been over grown with weeds when they first moved in. With Beulah's help, they grow vegetables and blueberries. The little extra money Bill makes, he gets from doing chores around the neighborhood.

"Hi, Mr. Jackson."

"Diego, what all ya'lls up to? I ain't seen you in days."

"Nuthin' much, Mr. Jackson. Picked up a dollar five downtown, today."

"You did? Now, how in tarnation did you do that? Missus Davina ain't paid me but twenty five cent to do all o' this here."

"With a lock. You know…the bubble gum thing."

"Oh…oh, oh…ya'll went fishin'. Yeah, I got ya. Well, ah needs to do somethin'. I gots to pay my 'lectric bill. It be two months late and the missus cayn't be without no 'lectric. And old Geezer the cat needs to eat, too. Momma been feedin' him scraps, but thems cats got to have theys meat, and I ain't seen a mouse in the house since the winter time. I do believe that little bugger went and et ever one of them critters."

"I can help you make a little money, Mr. Jackson."

"Ya'll can? Now how do you propose to do that, son? It's nice of you to offer, but you ain't nothin' but a young sprout yo-self."

"No…really Mr. Jackson, we can do it together."

"Bill!"

"Mr. Bill, sir. I know a lot of ways…"

"No, just plain Bill. Just call me Bill, okay, Diego?"

"Oh, sure."

"I'm sorry son, what was it ya'll was sayin', now?"

"Oh…uh…there are a lot of bus stops and subway stations I haven't even touched, yet. We can go partners, fifty, fifty on everything."

"Fifta, fifta? Well, that's mighty generous of ya'll."

Bill gave it a moment's thought. "You know what? I think it just might work. Heck, at this point, I'll tries anathang."

"Sure it'll work and I have a lot of other ways to make spare change, too."

Bill's arms folded across his chest as he looked warily at Diego. "Now, Is they legal son? You know…the good Lord…"

"No, really. It's all on the up and up. We can make lots of spare change."

"I believe you know what you're sayin', son. Our wallets are going to grow fatter than a happy tic in a barrel o' blood. Ain't that right, Mista Diego?"

"Ha ha! I sure hope so."

"Well…if'n you're a goin' to be ma partna, then you gots to come and meet momma for her approval. Is that okay with you?"

"Sure, Mr. Bill…, I mean Bill. I have to run home real quick first to drop off this milk, but I'll be right back."

"Takes your sweet time there, now. And say hello to your Momma for me. Ain't no rush, I got to finish up here, anyways."

Bergen Street is a narrow and busy roadway, too narrow for the two way street it is. Named after a Dutch settler back in the 1600's, the cobble stones beneath the street had long ago been paved over with asphalt. Here and there, where blacktop is missing, the stones show through.

This was also the Bergen Street trolley route. The bus was a hybrid cross on wheels that ran on power from electric lines overhead. Kids liked to hitch free rides on the back bumper. Diego even did that himself. Once in a while a kid would hold onto the pole ropes that connect the bus to the guide wires overhead, the source of the vehicle's power. Nothing but electric current held the connection together, and if too much weight was applied to the pole ropes, the connection separated and the bus lost power.

The driver, interrupted from his hypnotic trance on the double line, now had to exit the bus to reconnect the power. This was done by maneuvering the pole ropes to guide the shoes back onto the electric lines above the bus.

"That's Momma's place right there. It's the building next to that hallelujah church. Just listen to them a sangin' inside."

Nothing but a store front, the Pentecostal church door stood wide open and alive with song. Tambourines shook in energetic hands, with Spanish lyrics shouted loudly in unison. A few overzealous patrons had fallen to the floor and were either passed out or begging for salvation and exoneration for their sins.

"Come on in, son, meet old momma," said Bill, waving for Diego to enter the building next door. "Say, Momma, I got here a frien' o' mine."

Diego stepped down the three steps and passed through the outside door into a long hallway. Behind him, the door creaked closed with the help of a rusty spring which barely hung on to the wooden door like an afterthought. He followed Bill to the back end of the house and into the musty air of the Jackson's furnished room.

"Well now, who all we got here?" said a deeply wrinkled, kind faced Beulah. Her eyes smiled as she tried to focus through cataracts, her head, turned to the side for a better view.

"This here be Diego…ma frien' from Dean Street."

Beulah laid a washed dish on a towel, wiped worn hands on a plaid apron, and in a high pitched voice, said, "Dean Street? Well, I is pleased at meeting ya'll, Diega."

"Me too, ma'am. I mean…I'm pleased to meet you, too, Mrs. Beulah."

"Oh, shesh! Just Beulah, that's all. So, what're you doing hangin' 'roun' with this ol' troublemaka over here?"

"Bill wanted me to meet you, ma'am."

"We come to see you, that's all, Mamma," Bill said, in an apologetic sounding voice.

"Want some corn braid, Diega?"

"Sure ma'am."

"I'll puts some butter on it for ya. Well sit on down and set a spell," she said, with impatience.

Looking around, Diego picked the corner of a well-used couch and sank into it. Springs popped somewhere below, frightening a couple of roaches that fell from the bottom and then scurried across the floor.

"Comftable ain' it?" Beulah said. Papa found it right outside. I bet you it belonged to that church next doe, ain't that so, Mista Jackson?"

"Sho 'nough is, Missus Jackson."

Beulah crossed the multi flowered linoleum, though much of the pattern had long worn through. In places all that showed was the dull, reddish-brown base from the underside, and the imprint of the floor's wooden boards.

In the corner of the room, a bed, consisting solely of a mattress and box spring, lay neatly made up.

She handed Diego the corn bread on the only saucer that wasn't chipped.

"How come you ain't in school these days?"

"We're on vacation."

"Vacation? Wale ah'll be! I guess that's proper. Can't be all work and no play."

Bill interrupted. "We is a goin' into a partnership on er, a...a, a business ventcha."

"What kind a business ventcha you talkin' 'bout, Papa Jackson?"

"Work ventcha! We's is a goin' to have a root. Goin' to cover all of thems bus stops what's got them thare grating thangs peoples be standing on and dropping they change. Ain't that so, son?"

"That's right, Mr. Jackson. We're going to make some money and split it fifty, fifty," said Diego.

Beulah's eyes lit up. She energetically raised an arm up and slapped her thigh in jest. "Fifta, fifta? Well glory be! We all gonna be rich, now ain't we, Mista Diega?"

The boy caught Beulah's wink. "Well, ha ha, no, not exactly."

"How's that corn braid?"

"Real good, Mrs. Jackson. I mean, Beulah, ma'am."

"Here, take this piece on home with ya."

"You mind if I give it to my mom?"

"Well shucks no! Here's another piece...let me stick it in with the other one."

Two blocks away on Bond Street, Officer Bob Scanlon, huskily built with a pronounced belly and pocked face, turned the corner and headed up Dean Street. He's nearing Leroy's father, Thomas, who is in front of his house sweeping the sidewalk.

"Afternoon officer, good weather we got here today."

"Humph!" Scanlon kept looking straight ahead.

Thomas was left staring at the back of the cop's head as he passed by, and as usual, there had been no reply.

(frowning) Why do I bother?

Next door, Laura Swift emptied the mailbox at the top of the stoop and closed the lid. "Hi, Bob. I saw you at Saint Paul's Sunday. You were standing in the back of the church."

"How you doin', Laura, how's Joe?"

"Good! He's home early from work."

"That church sure was crowded yesterday. If you get there a minute late, you don't get a seat." Seeing Thomas go inside, Scanlon covered his mouth and softly growled, "The neighborhood's going to pot really fast. All this welfare moving in and the likes of people like him buying up the houses cheap. It sure ain't like it used to be."

"You're right, there, Bob. But he's not that bad for a colored man. I guess the Jamaicans might be a better quality, if you know what I mean?"

"Nah, they all suck. The jail's full of his kind. Them and the Puerto Ricans. If Hitler was here, he would know what to do with them."

"Well…I…I can't really say, I really don't mind so much, as long as they don't bother me."

"That's just it! You gotta nail everything down. They don't know how to live right. If it was up to me, I'd ship the whole lot of them back to Africa. And the Puerto Ricans, too. They can go back to their freakin' island. I don't trust none of 'em."

Laura kept her slight smile. "Well, eh…I…I don't really know what to…"

"Yeah, sure! Say hello to Joe for me."

"All right, Bob. Enjoy the good weather."

Approaching the corner, the cop crossed over to the other side of the street. He passed Diego at the broad sidewalk in front of D'avino's grocery while looking around for a violation. Neither one looked at the other.

Cow bells jingled behind as the cop entered the store. Standing on the scuffed, plank floor in the middle of the aisle, he stared at Mr. D'avino, who looked back worried from behind the counter.

"Well…where is it?" The cop demanded.

"Hey, looka, Officer a-Scanaleen…I'm a know I'm a late for the money, but you come a tomorrow and I feex everything."

"That ain't gonna fly with the captain and you know it."

"It's a okay. No worry. I'm a …"

"I'm a what? That envelope is supposed to be in my hand every Tuesday. Today's Wednesday, already. How come I don't have this problem with Herzog on the next block? How many times do we gotta do this?"

At that moment, Mrs. D'avino entered from the back room. "Pleasa, leava my husband alone. We pay tomorrow."

Scanlon scowled. He opened the red lid to the trunk shaped, Coca Cola fridge and pulled out a Yoo Hoo. He popped the bottle open from the machine's built-in bottle opener, with the cap dropping into a collector at the bottom. Taking a sip, he said, "One more day. Otherwise, we can't be responsible if somebody should break that nice big window and torch the place while you're sleepin'."

"Yes, offeecer. Tomorrow eeza no problem."

"Two o'clock! Don't' forget!"

***

"Ya'll got that gum?" Bill asked Diego."

"I sure do…and the lock."

An odd couple, the two made their way up Nevins Street---Bill, all of 6'4" and Diego, a chest level, 5'1".

Bill said, "That old Herzog's deli sure 'nough has lots o' customas. That's where the 'spensive stuff be, ham and all that. I don't neva go in that sto'. It is way too 'spensive for me."

"I go to the Italian grocery, myself," said Diego. "We don't buy much ham, hardly."

"Why? Dontcha likes it?"

"Well…yeah! Say, if we do real good today, you and I could buy a whole half pound of ham, right, Mr. Jackson? I mean, Bill."

"Sure son. We might end up buyin' all theys hams whats theys got in that ol' sto.'"

They both laughed at that.

"We can have a feast at my place," said Diego.

"Well now, that's a deal, but let's see how wees do fust. Can't be countin' no chickens before theys a hatches. Gotta watch out for that ol' fox, don't ya know. He always be hangin' 'round the coup when you're least expectin' it, and before ya knows it…**BAM!** He's got another chicken in his mouth. I still got that 'lectric bill to take care o', too, so I don't rightly knows about no ham. At least, not for a while."

It took the entire day to cover the rest of the gratings along that same side of Flatbush Avenue toward Grand Army Plaza. Minus the subway fare back, they netted; 31 tokens, 17 quarters, 12 dimes and 6 nickels. Three dollars and fifty three cents apiece---not a bad take for the first day out.

The following day they picked up where they left off, the other side of Flatbush Avenue where they worked their way back toward the bridges. By the end of the week, bill had half of his electric bill covered. Eventually, however, the subway gratings dried out.

"We needs to find another way to make money, Diego."

"I know and I've been kind o' thinking about that. If we can get our hands on an old baby carriage, we could make a wooden box for it and help people carry groceries home for a tip."

"Well, that's a fine idea. Now you're using that ol' grey stuff in that head o' yours. I'll get busy on the box."

"Okay, and I think I know where we can get us a carriage."

Wednesday 10:22 A.M.

(Clang! Bang! Crash!)

"Diego, wassup?" said Louie, from behind the garbage truck.

"Hi, Louie?" Diego turned toward the driver's window. "Anything today, Petey?"

"Yeah, hi kid. Nah! I ain't got nuttin' for you today, sorry."

"Oh, that's okay. Thanks anyway."

"Yeah, yeah."

Louie shouted at his partner. "Hey Fat Tony, get your head outa the freagin' bags, huh? Jeez! We ain't never gonna get finished. So, how's it going, Diego?"

"Real good, Louie. Say, do you guys ever find baby carriages?"

"Baby carriages? Who's gonna have a baby?"

"No! Nobody! I need it for myself."

"Aintcha kinda too young to be thinkin' about those things?"

"Oh…no, it's not for a baby. I need it to make money."

"Now, how are you gonna make money with a baby carriage? Hey, Fat Tony…you hear dis?"

"Yeah, I hoid," Fat Tony answered. "So what!"

"The kid needs a baby carriage. You had a bunch a dem bambino things yourself, didn't you, ha ha?"

Tony's head reemerged from deep inside a shopping bag. "Very funny. Yeah, sure, I'll look in my basement when I get home. I got a carriage down there somewhere. The Cadillac of carriages. You're gonna like that one if I find it, Diego."

"Thanks. Can you bring it Friday?"

"Yeah, yeah, I'll see. Friday…yeah sure."

Petey stuck his head out of the driver's window. "Ayyy! Does ya think we got all day? Let's go! We gotta get lunch! Stop your yakin' back there and finish up, will ya?"

Friday: Diego's Apartment 10:25 A.M.

"So, you are Mister Jackson. I'm so happy to meet you," said Ana, wiping her hand on a dish towel before extending it for a welcoming handshake.

"And I is pleased at meetin' ya'll, Missus Ana. Sure is a roomy place ya got here."

"Gracias."

Worried, Diego looked at his mother from across the table. "Tony says he's bringing me a carriage today, but I just don't know…he didn't seem like he…"

"The carriage you were telling me about? Don't worry. If Tony says he will bring it, then Tony will bring it. Have some coffee, Mister Jackson?"

"Thank ya kindly, Missus Ana."

She limped to the table and poured it for him. "Milk is on the table with the sugar."

"This is some strong coffee, Missus Ana."

"Mom makes it in a stinky old sock."

"No I don't. He's only joking. I use one of these."

Ana held up a cloth pouch with a wire frame around the opening and filled with Bustelo coffee grinds, a strong Spanish coffee. She put the pouch into a pot of boiling water to allow it to steep.

"I can give you bread with butter if you'd like?"

"No thank ya, ma'am. Ah just et. Thank you just the same, though."

VROOM…BANG…BAM!

"I guess that'd be them now," said Bill. "Let's go meet the boys, outside."

Diego ran down the steps two at a time and yelled over the truck noise. "Did you find anything, Tony?"

"Nah…I ain't found nuthin', right, Louie?" Tony asked.

"Nope!" said Louie. "Fat Tony ain't found nuthin' in the basement?"

Petey leaned his head out, took a puff from a freshly lit cigar and slipped a smile.

"Yeah, too bad, right, Fat Tony?" Louie repeated.

"Yup," Tony nodded back. "I looks and I don't see no carriage down there nowhere. Nope, nope…and then guess what happened?"

Diego shrugged.

"Well, I's comes to work this mornin' and I dunno, but I looks up at the pigeons flying 'round the garage and guess what I sees up dere? A freakin' carriage right on top a da truck. Ain't that right, Louie?"

"Yup, I seen it there myself. Take a look, kid."

The smile on the boy stretched wider. There on the roof of the truck sat a blue carriage with a cushy chrome spring above each wheel. Louie climbed up and handed it down to Tony.

"Here ya go, kid. It's all yours."

"Wow! Check it out, Bill," the boy said.

"That sure be a fancy one," the old gent, said.

"Ayyy…whose the mooly?" Petey quipped, in his usual husky voice.

"He's my friend and new business partner, Mr. Bill Jackson," Diego replied.

Petey smirked. "Mister who? …Oh! 'Scuse me! Mr. Jackson he says. Ho, ho!"

"Ah, shaddup, Petey." Louie snapped. "Mr. Jackson is his business partna and that's, that. Got it?"

"Yeah…yeah, sure. Okay, hot shot. Mr. Jackson it is. So what is it now… you guys are in the transportation business?" Without waiting for an answer, Petey waved them off and ducked back inside the cab.

"That's right," Louie shouted. "They're in the transportation business and that ain't no business of yours." He turned to Diego. "Lotsa luck kid."

"Yeah, that goes for me, too. Lotsa luck," said Fat Tony. "And you, too, Mr. Jackson."

"Thank ya, boys," said Bill. "That's right mighty nice of y'all fellas."

"Yo! Let's go! Lunchtime, remember?" Petey yelled.

Louie and Tony hopped onto the back of the hopper and waved as the garbage truck began to accelerate down the street.

Bill waved back. "They sho is some nice fellas. Come on, Diego. We all is a goin' to my place to puts the box onto this here carriage. We is goin' to make some mon-a-ay to-o-o…day?"

Beulah gave Diego a kiss on the forehead as soon as he entered the Jackson's room. In a high pitched voice, she said, "How be ma favorite Puerto Rica child."

"I'm fine Mrs. Jackson, thank you."

Eying the carriage in the hall, she said, "So is you all boys a goin' to put this thang togetha today?"

"Yes, ma'am, Diego answered."

Bill smiled. "She sho is a beaut, ain't she, Missus Jackson?"

"She sho is, Mista Jackson," Beulah assertively replied.

"I'll be right back," said Bill. "Now don't ya'll go nowhere, Diego."

"Now where all he gonna go when he's a settin' right here by me?" Beulah scolded. "Now go on with you and get that old box. Diega done wait long enough. You want some pa, Diega?"

"Pa?"

"Yes, suh! Blue berry pa. Let me git some fer ya. We picks the blue berries right from this here yard right out there in April and froze up a bunch of it."

The pie was delicious---finger scraping the plate delicious. Had Diego been home, he would have licked it clean.

Banging and huffing soon came from the hallway. The door opened and in Bill's arms was a large, blue wooden box.

"I paints this on here masalf. How you like it?"

BILL and D EGGO grossry diliverees

"Well? Whatcha thank? I did all o' this here letterin' masalf what ya'll sees here?"

"I think you should have let me do the lettering, Bill?"

"Aw, fiddlesticks, son. She's good 'nough. Are you ready to go to work?"

"Sure! We can still make the rush hour. That's when people buy stuff on their way home from work. Should we try Herzog's deli first?"

"Deli, smelly! Gee willikers, we is in the big times, Diego, so we got to think big! You and I is a goin' to the A and a P. That's where the big money is. Now, let's get on out there. Bye bye, Momma."

The Front of the A & P Supermarket

"We been here for a good half a hour and ain't nobody so much as give us a look see. Hey, hold on! Look over there, another one's a comin'!"

"She's awfully fat, Bill. I bet you she could use our help."

Look snappy son. Fix your shirt. Hurry up and tucks it in. You gots to look sharp if ya want to be in the big times."

"How's this? Does it look okay, now?"

"Boy, don'tcha ever combs your hair?" Bill caught himself, softened his voice and brushed Diego's hair back with long, caloused fingers. "Now go on and ask if she needs our help."

"Hello, ma'am. Can we help you with the groceries?"

"Excuse me?" the lady snapped. "I don't need anyone's help. Oh, the nerve. Now they have convicts trying to steal your groceries. What will they think of next?"

The lady turned her back to them and huffed off.

"Now, I'll be. Will you looky at that?" said Bill.

"I think she was afraid of you," Diego replied. "You know...you being big and all."

"Ya'll mean colored, dontcha, boy? Well, maybe. She sho be mad, though, wasn't she? Hey son, did you see that big ol' backside of hers?"

"Her what?" Diego giggled.

"She's got a butt bigger'en a forty dollar mule."

"A forty dollar mule?"

"Yes, suh! It'd take two trips with a wheelbarra to haul that butt on home. Hey, here come another one. Now, I'll stand ways over there like we ain't together. Let's see if that don't make no difference."

"Ma'am, do you need some help with the groceries?" Diego asked.

"Well, I only live a few blocks away. Well okay, sure. What do I do...put them in here?"

"I'll do it for you, ma'am."

"And what's your name?"

"Diego, ma'am."

"Well, nice to meet you, Diego."

Three blocks went by quickly. At the lady's front gate, Diego reached for the bags.

The lady turned back from looking behind her. "That man has been following us ever since we left the store. I just don't know, but I think he's up to no good."

"Don't worry. That's Bill. He's my partner."

"Humph! This is so irregular. Oh, here...take this and leave the bags right there next to the steps. I can bring them in myself. Goodbye!"

"Goodbye, ma'am."

He met up with Bill.

"How did we do, son?"

"A whole dollar."

"A dollar? Is that right?"

"I think she was so scared when she saw you following us, she didn't bother to look for change. I'm sorry, Bill, but I'm not so sure this delivery thing is going to work out in the long run."

"So now you is a thankin' that maybe this here business went on belly up like a shot up gator?"

"Well, yeah, that's exactly what I was thinking...sorta. We spent all of our time getting this carriage together for nothing."

"Now don't go sellin' your mule to buy a cow."

"Ha! No, but you know what? I may have another idea."

"What's your idea, son, 'cause ah can't think o' one as easily as you can? Ever' time I stands up, my mind sits down."

"We can shine shoes in front of the Fox Theatre."

"Oh...now ah knows how to shine shoes. I goes way-y-ys back on thata one. Spit Shine Bill, that's what they used to call me. Now, I can teach ya'll a thang or two right there."

Diego scratched his chin. "Let's not spit on nobody's shoes, Bill. It might make them mad."

***

Scanlon continuously twirled a night stick around his wrist, two to the left and then two to the right as he approached the corner of Nevins and Dean. At D'avino's grocery, he pushed the door open and waited for a customer to leave. From a cooler at the back wall, he removed a six pack of Piels. As soon as the lady left, he set it on the counter. "Put this in a paper bag along with the envelope."

Mr. D'avino did as he was told and slid the bag toward him.

"How much is in the envelope?"

"Fifty dollars as usual."

"Fifty? No…no…no! You owe interest! You're two days late. What did you think, you'd get away with that for nuthin'? Put another ten in there."

"But, offeecer…where a we gonna getta this money?"

"In that fuckin' register, that's where. Don't play around with me."

Officer a Scaleen, I no have a notheeng left. All day I'm a payza the bills, the milk truck, the newzapaper guy, the soda truck. There's a notheeng left."

"Then go find it. I'm not leavin' until you do."

Scanlon stepped hard to the front of the store and flicked the lock. He turned the "Closed" sign around so that it faced the outside and lowered the blinds. "Go on! Go get it! What're you waitin' for?"

The store owner cowered to the back room and stood next to his wife at the kitchen table. "He's a crazy. Now he wants another ten. We're we a gonna geta this money?"

Mrs. D'avino shook her head. "The church money! What choice do we have?"

Reluctantly, he reached for a coffee tin on top of the refrigerator, emptied it out on the table and began to count out a five, three singles and eight quarters. He glanced at his wife, pressed his lips together and returned to the front of the store.

"Put it in the bag with the rest," said Scanlon. He let himself out and headed to the next stop, a fish store on Bergen Street. The ten, he put in his wallet.

Chapter Three
Friends

The rest of the summer was prosperous for the B & D partnership. Bill and Diego learned more ways to increase their earnings. They mowed lawns, painted fences and did anything and everything to make a buck. It was enough for Diego to set aside money for school clothes. For the first time in years, Bill was able to put a little away in savings for Beulah and himself.

And it wasn't all work and no play. Diego involved old Bill in a lot of the things he did, like stick ball. It was on a particularly hot day when…

"We need two more players," said Larry, "The Chubs" Constantine, a chunky kid from down the block.

"Who said you were playing?" said Thomas' son, Leroy. "I need two good players for first and third."

"I can play first," said Diego.

"No! I need you to play second so you can cover anything that goes up the middle. No one else can catch as good as you around here."

The Pacific Street Lions, the opposing team from the next block, sat on a stoop getting frustrated with the wait.

Charlie, their lead hitter, shouted annoyingly at Leroy. "You know what, your team was supposed to be next up to play us, so where the hell are your players?"

"Don't worry," said Leroy.

Leroy's dad, Thomas, owned a dump truck and worked six days a week. Besides Leroy, he raised the boy's two older brothers and a sister. His brothers were both away in college. His sister was studying nursing.

"We'll get the players! Sit tight! We're coming right back."

In a huddle, the team explored their options, which was zip at the moment.

"Where are we gonna get two more players?" said Leroy. "And what ever happened to our star player, Hector, by the way?"

"He had to go with his parents," said Diego.

"Maybe they're back by now. Where did they go?"

"Out to Jersey someplace."

"That don't do us no good," Larry replied.

Diego said, "If we forfeit this game, we can't play the championship, and right now we're in a good spot for that. We could've beaten those Lions, hands down."

"Yeah, we could have," said Leroy. "Without Hector, though, I don't know what we're gonna do."

Diego looked up. "Wait a sec! Nobody said we had to be kids, right?"

"Whaddya mean?" interrupted, Joey, "The Mez" Marcantonio, one of the outfielders.

"Yeah, exactly!" said, Diego. "Who says we can't have a grown man on the team." He turned toward the Lions and shouted, "Hey Charlie! We'll be right back!"

"Five minutes, or ya forfeit the game," Charlie yelled.

"Where'd you get that rule from?" The Chubs retorted.

"Yeah, Charlie, you gotta give us more time," said Leroy.

"Okay, fifteen minutes. If you're not back by then, we're leavin'."

"What for? We can beat you with the guys we have," yelled Jose, "The el Paso kid".

"Yeah, sure…right!" Charlie fumed. "Come on Butchie, let's get a coupla sodas."

Leroy's entire team, the Dean Street Kings, waited outside Bill Jackson's building on Bergen Street while Diego and Leroy went inside.

"Well, uh, ah ain't played no baseball in years…and stickball no less. Nope, ah ain't never played no baseball with no stick."

"You don't have to bat. We need someone for first or third base? Are you any good?" Leroy asked.

"I was a fair player in ma day. Ah thank so."

"Then you'll play?"

"Ain't nothin' else 'roun hear to do. Momma's a bit tarred. It'd be good for her to rest up a bit. That okay with you, Mama?"

"Go have fun with the boys, Papa Jackson," Beulah said.

Fine, boys! Let's go!"

"You're sure you're up to this, now?" said Leroy.

"Yeah, how do you feel?" Diego worried. You're not tired or anything, are you, Bill?"

"Oh, hell no! I'm as fit as a fiddle. In fact, I feel happier than a twister in a trailer park."

Diego and Leroy grinned at one another.

"We need one more guy, but I can't think of anybody else that we can get in five minutes," said Diego.

Bill replied. "Oh, ah can, and I know he's a darn good player, 'cause he plays on a baseball team in Bensonhurst."

Back on Dean Street, Charlie made no effort to conceal his laughter as soon as he saw Diego exit the corner grocery with the store owner and Bill Jackson trailing behind with the rest of the team.

"Hey, man! Is that the two champion players you're gonna play us with," he scoffed.

"Don't worry about us, we're ready," said the Chubs.

Another huddle formed as the Dean Street Kings bent into a tight circle. Bill wrapped his tall frame around Mr. D'avino and Diego.

"What position can you play, Mr. D?" asked Leroy.

"I eeza plays alla the positia. Which a one you wanta me to play?"

"We really need someone on third."

Then I playza third. Where's a you bases?"

Leroy pointed them out. "The front fender of the black Buick is first. The manhole is second, and third is the back fender of that Studebaker. If a runner tags any of those, he's safe."

"So where's a you home base?"

"That little pothole right behind you, Mr. D?"

"That's a good. Say...watsa the name of you boyza team?"

"The Dean Street Kings."

"I'm a gotcha Leroy. Let's go and plays a the ball."

Bill covered first base, or fender, while Diego, a.k.a. "The Whiz", took second. Right field was covered by Jerry "The Giraffe" Muldoon, the tallest kid there. Jimmy "Jiminy Cricket" Lanahan worked left field. Also in the outfield was Joey "The Mez" Marcantonio. He's there to back up the other two fielders, or to catch anything that falls short through the trees. Whatever landed beyond the gates and into the front yards was foul and counted as a strike, of which a batter was allowed only two. Home plate, or the pothole, was covered by "Island Mon" Leroy, the captain of the team.

Larry "The Chubs" Constantine and Jose "The el Paso Kid" Avila sat in reserve. The Chubs sits there because he can't hit for shit, nor catch anything but a fever. Jose, on the other hand, is the team's best hitter. Leroy wants him to rest his hitting arm for when he really needs him. He doesn't want a replay of previous games when Jose burned out just when the team was taking a dive. Without Hector, it was a chance he would have to take.

From inside the Lion's huddle, Charlie had something he wanted to say. "I doubt if those two ol' farts can even run. They don't have Hector, so this is gonna be a piece o' cake. When the old guys get to bat, make sure you all move in, you hear?"

"Yeah, like they're gonna get a hit in the first place," Butchie quipped.

The game went well for the Lions. By the fifth inning they were ahead by three runs.

At the bottom of the fifth, with two on base, Mr. D'avino grabbed the bat for the Dean Street Kings. He played baseball all his life, but had a hard time hitting a pink rubber ball with a bat that was no more than an inch thick.

"Come on Mr. D, get a homerun," Larry shouted.

"Donta you worry. I'm a think I gotta the hang of it thisa time."

Butchie shouted to him, "Yeah, Grandpa, like you did the last two times at bat, right? Ha, ha!"

"Aw, shut up Butchie," The Chubs boldly yelled.

"You gonna make me?" Butchie shouted, taking a couple of steps toward Larry before two teammates stopped him.

Butchie's dad is a member of an Irish gang of thugs that make their money through extortion. They control all of downtown Brooklyn and have no affiliation with the Irish "Hell's Kitchen" gang in Manhattan other than an amicable association.

Waiting for their turn at bat, Bill said to Diego, "That boy out there is as sharp as a bowling ball."

"And that isn't very sharp, right, Bill?" Diego replied, chuckling.

"Not very…and not only that, if his brains was gas, he wouldn't have enough to run a go cart 'roun' a Cheerio."

Diego liked the old man, but once Hector was back, convincing Leroy to keep him on the team would be another matter.

"Come on, what are you guys waitin' for?" Charlie yelled. "Let's play!"

Mr. D'avino tossed the ball into the air, let it bounce once and gave it all he had.

Larry shouted, "That's a tip ball. That don't count, Mr. D, you go again." Larry liked calling the shots. He liked it even better than playing the game.

Again, Mr. D'avino tossed the ball up, let it bounce and swung.

"You missed Grandpa. Maybe you better sit down and rest awhile," said one of the Lion's.

"That's right! Maybe you better retire," another said, followed by more snickering. "One more and you're out!"

What no one there knew was that Mr. D'avino was once a minor league player back in Italy. At the time he was voted most valuable player three years in a row. He also played well for the Bensonhurst team here in Brooklyn with mostly older Italians like himself, but that was hardball.

Setting himself, Mr. D took his time and then tossed the ball into the air.
BOUNCE...WHACK

As everyone there gaped open mouthed, the pinky sliced left and sailed over the tops of the trees two thirds of the way to Bond Street on the next corner. It surprised them all, all of them except for Mr. D'avino, of course.

"Holy shit! man, I ain't never seen a ball hit that far," Butchie said. "And never by an old man, neither!"

Charlie yelled, "Damn! A home run and two already on base. Crap! Now the scores even, tied up five to five. I don't believe this is happening."

Diego addressed Bill. "Did you know that back in '55, Willie Mays used to spend his spare time playing stick ball with the kids up in the Bronx?"

"Wasn't that before he went into the Army?"

"Yes, when he played with the Giants. Well...he used to be known as a four sewer hitter. Now, that's about two city blocks, isn't it, Bill?"

"Sho is. He's a southern boy, too. Birmingham!"

"Birmingham? Where's that?"

"Alabamy."

Bill, also, was unstoppable when he covered first base. Nothing the Lions hit his way got past him. And he had no problem catching Jerry's fast ball thrown all the way from outfield. By the bottom of the ninth they were still at a five to five stalemate.

"When are you going to let Jose hit," Larry screamed.

"Right now," said Leroy.

"It's about time!" said Diego.

As he scanned the opposing team, Diego envisioned the heavy steel doors of a barn opening wide to unleash the prize bull. Riding on the bull's shoulders was Senor Jose, the El Paso Kid, a bat in his grip.

"Do it, Jose! Remember the Alamo!" Larry yelled.

For the last fifteen minutes, Jose had done nothing but loosen up and swing his custom made bat through the air. The broom stick was cut at exactly the right length with Jesus Christ painted on the top of it between two, blue bands to represent heaven. At the business part of the bat where the stick met the ball, a black, snorting bull with red eyes stood ready to charge. Brown tarantulas, black scorpions and green, prickly pear cacti adorned the rest of it.

Waiting to score on third was Jiminy Cricket. On second, the Giraffe towered over the manhole like a street light.

At the forefront of the pothole and as cool as an illegal swimming across the cold Rio Grande, the El Paso Kid, a normally quiet sort, smiled and pointed his bat toward Bond Street. "Kiss this ball goodbye, suckers."

"Fuck you, Jose," Butchie shouted. "You couldn't hit a refried bean off the tip of your nose with your finger."

"Stop cursing, Butchie," Diego scolded. "Can't you see there's little kids out here?"

"Yeah, right! Like that's somethin' they haven't heard before."

Jose wet his forefinger and stuck it in the air. "Three degrees to the left and forty five degrees high…no problem."

"Aw, stop the bullshit, beano," Butchie yelled.

Jose bounced the pinky against the pavement. He had his own style. Once set, he liked to let the ball bounce twice before swinging. The added second allowed more time to nail it just right. Jose knew he could make Bond Street, the goal was to not hit the ball foul. He took a full breath and stretched his batting arm. He swung the stick in a wide circle a few times, laid it across his right shoulder and tossed the ball into the air.

Somewhere very distant, in a place about two thousand miles to the southwest of Brooklyn and deep inside the Lone Star State, a powerful, snorting bull raked its hooves into the dry Texas dust.

BOUNCE…BOUNCE…SLAM

"Holy burritos! How the hell did he do that?" Butchie shrieked as he watched the ball sail well above the trees and clear across Bond Street.

Charlie's head lowered. He rubbed his neck and swallowed the lump in his throat. "Welp, I guess that's the game fellas."

With their arms wrapped around one another, Jimminy Cricket and the Giraffe feigned two girls as they swayed sashaying hips toward home plate. The casual walk home was a long drawn out affair---the top of Jimmy's head barely reaching the bottom of Jerry's chest. It was a comical sight, 'though not so for the Lions.

Jimmy ethereally waved a delicate hand through the air and effeminately said, "Tsk! Tsk! Oh, Jeremiah, you don't suppothe we hurt the feelings of those two little boys over there, do you?"

Jerry checked behind at Butchie and Charlie, and with the best impersonation of Marilyn Monroe he could muster, eagerly chimed in. "Oh, I do hope so, my dear Jimmy. Too bad, isn't it?"

Reaching the pothole, the pair hovered over home plate momentarily.

"Oh, Jeremiah?"

"Yes, dear Jimmy?"

"Should I touch home, first?"

"Oh please do, you thilly savage, you."

Jimmy gently dipped his right toe beyond the top edge of the pothole.

"Tsk! Tsk! Oh, it tickles. There, Jeremiah…now you."

"How exciting. Now don't let me fall in that awful hole. Heeeere I go. Oh deary me."

To make it all legal, Jerry touched the edge of the pothole, while at the same time, The El Paso Kid walked home.

In the middle of all the happy faces, Mrs. D'avino poured cream soda in paper cups for each of the boys. Beulah passed out her home baked, chocolate chip cookies. It was a great day for the Kings as they each slapped five with their two, new rooky players. For a long time afterwards, it would be a game no one would forget.

***

The following morning, Sunday, Diego gathered in front of his stoop with Larry, Jerry, Jose and Jimmy.

"I'm super ready. I got my bathing suit on right now," said Larry.

"Me, too," said Jerry.

"Nah! Mine's in the bag," Jose chimed in. "I'll change when I get there. I'm not wearin' a wet bathing suit home."

"How much money do we have between us?" asked Diego.

Jimmy checked. "I ain't got but a token on me."

Larry searched his pockets. "I have a quarter, but I'm saving it for the movies. Why? Whaddya need money for?"

"I figured we put our money together to get a pizza later on," said Diego. "We're gonna be awfully hungry. Remember the last time?"

Jose shook his head and grinned. "Yeah, when Larry ate that half eaten chocolate bar he found in the street?"

Jerry laughed. "I remember that. It had ants crawling all over it and he hogged it all. Not that I would've eaten any."

"Hey, I brushed the ants off first," Larry retorted. "You wanted a piece too, Jerry. You was droolin' all over me. Don't you remember?"

"Ha, ha, that's right. Jerry wanted some, too. He even begged you for it," said Jimmy.

Jerry pushed him. "Aw, shut up, man."

Bill waved from across the street. "Fine game we had yesterday, wasn't it?"

Diego shouted. "Hey, do you want to go swimming with us?"

"Aw shit, Diego! What'd you go and do that for?" Larry grumbled.

"Swimmin'? Where at y'all boys goin' to go swimmin'?"

"Pier 34! Same place we always go. Come on...go with us!" said Diego.

"Wale...I ain't got no bathin' suit."

"So, go in with your jeans," said Jerry, waving Bill over. "They'll be dry by the time you get home, Mr. J."

"It sho be a hot one out here. Sho 'nough is. Jest give me a minute whiles ah puts this broom back."

The long walk toward the piers took them to the end of Dean Street where the name changed to Amity. They continued through the northern-most end of the Italian neighborhood of Carol Gardens on their left. To the right, a mix of Scandinavian, Polish and Irish families occupied the surrounding streets and had for generations. Among them, newly arrived Syrians huddled mostly on Pacific Street, between Court and Henry.

Mr. Jackson and the boys continued down Atlantic Avenue toward the river. At the very end, a fence blocked their way so they stayed on Furman

Street, walked about a half mile and turned left. The side street soon changed to a gravel road which continued over the water in the form of a pier supported by pilings. A weather faded sign before it read:

PIER 34

NO TRESSPASSING

Driven deep into the mud during the thirties and the hustle bustle days of factories and unchecked growth, the piers along the Brooklyn side of the East River now stood as forlorn monuments to that lost and prosperous past.

Bill shook his head at all of the broken glass and debris scattered about. Clumps of grass and dandelions maintained a stronghold inside any unclaimed crack in the sidewalk. The smell of creosote permeated the air. Another odor coming from the river smelled stale with a hint of decay. A thin, rainbow hew of oil floated on the surface. Bobbing in the shallow ripples was a condom floating like an expired sea slug, its mouth left agape as if from its final death throws. Long abandoned, rusty barges lined many of the other piers with sumac trees growing out of fractures. Empty warehouses, most of the windows broken, lined the surrounding blocks. Strewn about their empty lots were stripped cars of almost every conceivable make and size, the doors and engines missing from many of them. Across the sidewalks and cobblestone street were bald tires, fenders and chrome trim along with broken bottles.

"My, my, and another o' my. This here ain't 'zactly Holler Crick back at ol' Stenson's farm."

"This is a great spot," said Jose. "You can even see the Statue of Liberty."

"So this here be ya'll boy's swimmin' pool?"

"Ain't it great?" said Larry, splashing water at Jimmy.

"Boys...you can stick a cat into the oven, but that sho don't make it a biscuit."

"There's Manhattan!" said Jerry.

"Yes, suh! I sees it. An' right there be the Brooklyn Bridge, ain't that so?"

"The Staten Island Ferry! Over that way, Mr. J!"

"So it is, Jerra. I ain't never been on that boat."

"It only cost a token...fifteen cents."

"Fifteen cent? Is ya'll sho?"

"Yes, fifteen, that's all it is," said Larry.

"Wale, I do believe me an' the missus might just' take us a cruise on that ol' boat."

"If you don't get off, you can go back to Manhattan for free." Diego said. "I'll go with you."

"Me, too," Jose added.

"When is ya'll goin' in that water, Diego? You is as dry as a bum settin' outside a closed bar on a Sunday mornin'."

"I'm waiting for you, Bill!"

"Me! Hell, Ah sho don't wanta swallow up none of that there water none."

"Why?" said Larry. "I see ducks in here all the time. And people fish here, lots of people come to fish…even at night."

"That so? Does you ever see them fish aglowin' all green like? That right there could be a clue."

"Ha! No, really, lots of ducks hang around here."

"Funny, I don't see nary a one."

"Tides out," said Larry, "that's why."

"What y'all boys don't know, is if'n thems ducks you be claimin' to see, be the same ones that were there the day befo'. They might o' glowed just like them fishes you was talkin' 'bout and been a settin' all sick like at the bottom of that river a quackin' for they's momma."

Diego stood on top of a piling where he scanned the river and its banks.

Below his feet all he saw was the wooden deck of a Spanish galleon. Foamy white caps lapped abreast and washed over the forecastle, rocking the mighty ship from side to side. Below the distant horizon, in the final fiery glow of sunset, the fierce bow of an English brigantine chased through the waves to find him.

Diego, the pirate, drew an ornate saber from its sheath, the glistening reflective light, sweeping across the oak planks like a flash of lightening. He ordered the helmsman to come about and shouted to make ready the ship's canons---a double row of 40 carronades---32 pounders, scavenged from an English warship.

"Hey, you guys know about the kid that drowned out here last year?" he asked.

"What kid?" said Jerry.

"Yeah, what kid?" Larry wanted to know.

"A kid dove off one of these piers near here…and you know those big, metal milk cans?"

"Like the ones they use at the Borden Dairy down the street from us?" Bill asked.

"Yeah, only it was a four foot one. Well, the can was under the water sitting upright at the bottom and when the kid dove in, his head hit the can with so much force, it went right inside. It was wedged in so tight, he couldn't pull it back out."

Larry found that frightening. "Did he drown?"

"Well, whaddya think, stupid," Jose barked.

Larry shook his head vigorously. "I'm not diving, that's all. I'll go in, but I'm not diving. The heck with that. Hey Jimmy! I'm swimming to the end of the pier."

"I'll beat ya," Jimmy yelled.

Bill walked to the end to meet them and to watch the ferry make its way against the tide toward its berth at Battery Park.

Jerry came alongside.

Bill said, "I thought ya'll was still in the water, Jerra?"

"I'd rather stand here with you, Mr. Jackson. I like looking across the river at all those skyscrapers in Manhattan. The way they seem to come up right out of the water like that…that's really cool."

"Is you never been on that ferry nayther?"

"Nope! My mother doesn't go anywhere."

"What about yo' dadda?"

"He works a lot of hours. I don't see him much and when I do he's either on his way to work, or on his way to bed."

"Ah see what you mean. Wale…you can go with us when we take the cruise. Ya'll want to come?"

"Wow! That would be great, Mr. J. I'll ask my mom."

"Ya'll do that, son. Let me know, ya hear? Now doncha swaller up non o' that there water."

Tall and lanky, the sight of Jerry running to jump in seemed comical. Bill didn't laugh.

Now that's a nice boy.

"Aren't you going in," said Larry, wiping the brackish water from his eyes.

"No, son, but I sees that Jimmy beat you to the end."

"That's because I let him."

Jimmy smirked. "You're a sap, Larry. I beat you fair and square and you know it. Watch me beat him back, Mr. J."

The afternoon went by quickly. By late afternoon, everyone had built up an appetite. On the way home, they started to take the same streets, but turned right onto Clinton for no better reason than to go a different way. They were soon walking through the Italian neighborhood of Carol Gardens.

"This is a nice neighborhood," said Jose.

With the cool down of late afternoon, and it being Sunday, there were a lot of people outside sitting on stoops to get away from the heat of hot apartments. Large trees gave ample shade and everyone seemed to know one another. Folks sat at tables filled with snacks and liquid refreshments or leaned over fences in conversation.

"That guy over there keeps staring at us," said Larry.

"So don't look at him," said Diego.

Jimmy turned from looking at the same guy. "You know what? There's a couple of guys talking to him right now, and they're all looking this way."

This time Diego took a look. "Keep walking and don't turn around anymore."

"Boys, now don't pay'm no never mind and they won't trouble us none."

Bill couldn't have been more wrong. He and the boys turned the corner with the intention of returning to Amity, the same street they first took on the way to the piers. Walking along busy Court Street, they heard loud voices coming from behind. They grew louder as four teenage thugs caught up to them. One of the boys had a chain wrapped around his arm and as he spoke, unraveled it.

"So what were you assholes doin' on my street back there? You don't live here. None of youz do."

"We're walkin' back from the piers...that's all," said Diego.

"Oh yeah? Well you shoulda went a different way...and whose the coon with ya?"

"That's Bill, the cop," Larry blurted out. "He's escorting us to the precinct."

"Precinct? You fat piece o' lard. The precinct is way over dataway."

Jimmy cut in. "Look guys, we're not bothering nobody."

"Oh, no? Well guess what? We're bodderin' youz!"

The bully stepped back and started to swing the chain in a wide circle.

With Jimmy standing out front, the boy was in danger.

"Boys! Now, that there ain't necessara." Bill knew he could take the kid---knock him out with one punch. And he was sure, in his younger days, he could have taken all four, but hitting any of them would send the whole Italian neighborhood down on them. Instead, he got in front of Jimmy and motioned for him to stay back with a wave of his hand. At the same time, the troublemakers standing with the chain wielding kid raised their fists all set to fight.

Readying the chain for a swing at Bill, the bully said, "So...what're you gonna do, now, you old man?"

"That's enough, Nunzio!" said a huskily built man walking up behind him. "Get back home where you belong." His large hand encircled the chain wielding kid's neck and pushed him in the direction he wanted him to go. "Go ahead... get outta here. You too, the four of ya...get lost."

"You ain't heard da last of dis, Louie. I'm tellin' my father."

"Go ahead, Nunzio, and I hope he beats the crap out of you."

The four boys walked away as fast as they could back to President Street.

Bill and the rest couldn't believe their eyes.

Diego, impressed, blurted out, "Louie, what are you doing here?"

"Hey, I'm just your neighborhood garbage guy coming to the rescue."

"Louie, I sure is glad to see you."

"My pleasure, Mr. Jackson. And how about you, kid? Are you all right?"

"I'm okay, thanks."

"That's good! What's your name?"

"Jimmy!"

"Please to meet you, Jimmy."

"Louie, this is Jerry," Diego said. "This is Jose, and that's Larry."

"Larry, Jose, Jerry...please to meet all o' you guys. I saw ya's back on President and tried to catch up, but youz were already up the block and dat creep was followin' ya. Nunzio's da neighborhood trouble maker. I'll make sure I tell his father. I know Patsy, he doesn't put up with that kind of behaviour? Why, if he ever said anything to my wife and kids, I'd knock the block off his stupid shoulders, and that'd be without his father's permission."

"You probably don't have to worry about that, Louie. At least she's Italian," said Diego.

"No, she ain't! Yolanda is Puerto Rican."

"You're kidding, right?"

"No, why would I kid about that? Yeah, she's Puerto Rican, but I don't think of it that way. I never did. In fact, she was raised right there on President, down the block from me. And that's before the likes of doze guys were ever born. She knows everybody around here and they don't really care, anyways, except for a few dumb guidos that I wouldn't have nuttin' to do wit, no-hows. Heck, I knew her since I was dis high. So where were you all coming from?"

"Swimmin'," Bill said. "We were at the piers since this morning."

"I hope dem guys didn't scare youz too much."

"I wasn't scared," said Larry.

"Oh, sure!" Jose retorted. "Maybe you better check your underwear before you say anything else."

"How about you, Mr. J? You didn't seem scared at all," said Jerry.

"Well, then, ah guess ah fooled all o' ya'll, cuz ah was 'bout as nervous as a long tailed cat in a room full o' rockin' chairs.

Louie said, "Hey, you guys must be hungry. Come on, I'm gonna treat all o' you to pizza."

"Gee…you don't have to do that," said Diego.

"Yeah, Louie, it's okay, we'll be all right," said Jimmy. "Right, Larry?"

Larry rubbed his stomach and looked as if he was going to faint. "Man, I'm hungry!"

Louie put an arm around his shoulder. "That's it! You're all coming with me."

Two doors up, Rinaldi's Pizzeria stood out like a welcoming cafe. Outside, red cabana awnings shaded metal tables covered with green, well ironed table cloths.

"Grab a table boys." Louie opened the door and yelled inside. "Hey Ant'ny, get us three large pizza's and soda for all the boys."

"Louie, this is great! I don't know how to thank you for all of this," said Diego.

"What're friends for, right, Mr. Jackson?" Louie asked.

"Jus' call me Bill."

Louie's head was already back in the doorway shouting at Anthony. "Ya got anymore o' dem zepolis? Maybe Mr. Jackson and the boys want somethin' to munch on while they're waitin'."

From the kitchen, in the back of the restaurant, a voice sharply answered him. "Holda backa you horses, I'll be right outta there. Aspettare uno momento."

A short and very round Anthony, wearing an apron spotted with dried tomato sauce, soon weaved his way around the tables with a large tray of zepolis sprinkled generously with confectioner's sugar.

"Ant'ny, these are my friends from the garbage route. That's Mr. Jackson, he's the boss of all of them. Ha ha. Hey Larry, you're still all wet. What happened?"

"I had to put my clothes on over my bathing suit."

"I done that before many times, myself."

Anthony, on returning inside, immediately popped his head back out with an afterthought. "I'm a come out witha the pizza right away. You boyza come anytime you like to my pizza store. Anthony maka the besta pizza in a the whole of Brookaleen."

Louie grimaced. "Ayyy...Ant'ny! Pu-leeze! Dominick's always has a line around the block."

"So go to Domineek's. Why you coma over to this a place if a you like thatta one so much?"

"That's 'cause I feel sorry for you Ant'ny."

"Yeah, a you sorry lika a the hole inna my head. That Domineek, he's a from a the mountains in Italy. What does he know about how to make a good a pizza. They gotta nothing but sheep uppa they. All they know eeza how to make the cheese, that's all. So go you selfa to Domineek's!"

"Nah! I like the awning. Gets me outta the sun. You know wud I mean, Ant'ny?"

"Ah, stai zitto. Some a bullshit you are. You know whata you can scratch, huh, Louie?"

Louie banged on the table. "Hey where's the soda? Bring the soda! Come on! What kind of a pizza joint is this, anyway? Where's the service around here, huh?"

"Holda you horses. I'm a go get it righta now." Anthony's voice trailed off as he reentered the pizzeria.

"That Ant'ny's a good guy," Louie said. "I went to school with his son. Tough story, that one. Anyway, he ain't around no more."

"Why's that?" Bill asked.

Hold the fort, Bill. I'll be write back. I have to see a man about that horse Ant'ny was talkin' 'bout. I'll tell you when I get back."

To Bill's surprise, after Louie went inside to use the bathroom, a black kid of about eighteen and wearing a full apron, bumped the restaurant door with his rear end while carrying three large pizza's on aluminum trays. The boy had about him an air of confidence gained from having served many a table. He laid the first tray down in front of Larry. The other two, wedged between his finger tips and shoulder, were placed side by side in front of Bill and Jerry.

"Hi, I'm Louis! You guys aren't from around here are you?"

"No, and you ain't naytha, is you?" Bill queried.

"Well, these days I am. I live up stairs. Hey, I'm Louis. Enjoy the pizza. I'll be right back." The boy went inside as light footed as he came out.

Louie returned. "Now that looks good! I can see that you're enjoyin' it, too. Who brought it out...Luigi?"

"Why, no!" said Bill. "A young fella named Louis."

"Oh, that's Luigi. It's not his real name, but that's what Ant'ny calls him. He sorta adopted him. The kid has his own apartment upstairs. Used to live in Ant'ny's house a coupla of years ago, but he wanted his own place. Ant'ny owns the building, so it wasn't a problem."

"He seems like a nice kid," said Bill.

"Luigi? A piece o' cake. They get along priddy good, those two. Ant'ny calls him his Siciliano."

Just then the door opened. Louis, with two trays of veal parmesan, set them down at a different table. After a short conversation with the customers sitting there, he returned. "Anybody need anything else?"

Louie grabbed him by the wrist, "No, nothin'. Come sidown for a while. Take a load off your feet, you're makin' me dizzy wid all a this runnin' around."

"Well, I guess I can sit for a minute. How's everything with you, Louie?"

"I'm good. I was tellin' them how much of a trouble maker you are, you big eggplant."

Anthony stepped outside to join them. It's a so nice out here. Not lika before. Boy, what a hot day today. I see you boysa meet a my Luigi."

Standing alongside him, Anthony patted the boy lightly on the side of his face. Luigi eeza the besta partner I'm a ever have."

Louis shyly answered him. "What partner? I work for you, Anthony."

"Nah! Hogwasha! You anda me, we eeza partnas. Luigi here is a the best. I'm a surprise he's sitting down."

"I made him sit. You work him too hard," said Louie.

"He's a work he selfa too hard. I don't tella heem no theeng."

"The minestrone, did you check it?" Louis asked.

"Oh…go see, lika gooda boy."

"I heard you're goin' back to Italy to retire," said Louie.

"Si, maybe inna few more of the years."

"So, what about this place?"

"I eeza gonna give it to Luigi, cheap. The whola the building. I don't wanna theesa headache when me and the wife we go back to Italy."

"That's nice of you Ant'ny. He'll do good. He's a hard worker."

"That he is. Thees building taka care of heem for the whola his life. Hey, I gotta go inside. Enjoyza the pizza."

"That's what Mr. Herzog once told me."

"What's that, Diego?" Louie asked.

"That's how a lot of people in the city make a living. They work and save enough to buy a three story building with a store like this when they're still young. Like that fish market across the street, the owner in there could have been a fisherman, so maybe he doesn't want to go out to sea anymore and instead wants to stay home with his family. So, he buys a building and opens up a fish store, see?"

"Yeah, or maybe he just likes fish," said Larry.

"Right, or like the guy in that hardware store down the block, maybe he likes tools, so he opened up a…"

"So If I like candy, I could open a little candy store, right?" said Larry.

"That's the idea. You wouldn't have to take a subway to work, because you live upstairs. That's how a lot of people in the city make a living. Or a liquor store, a bar, or any kind of store, really. You work hard, live in one of the apartments, collect rent from somebody on the top floor, and the building takes care of you."

"Yup, I'd rent out the top floor, too. I wouldn't want to climb all those stairs, all the time," said Larry.

"I'm opening up a pet shop," Jose said, excitedly.

"Me too," said Jimmy. "That was my idea, first."

"Oh, yeah…well don't put your smelly store next to mine."

"Why not?"

"Because! I don't want you stealing my customers."

Diego shook his head. "That's not how it works, Jimmy. To make money, you have to open your store down the street far enough away so that you can serve the customers in that neighborhood. Get it?"

"Oh! I get it," said Larry. "That's why we see the same kind of stores like a mile down the street."

"Exactly," said Diego. "Me and mom are opening up a cuchifrito restaurant."

"A coochy coo, what?" Bill asked.

"Spanish food. We'll sell it to all of the Puerto Ricans."

"I'll be the first to try it," said Louie. "I like Rican food."

"What about me? Arentcha comin' to my store?" said Larry. "I give away free candy."

"How are you going to make money, if you give away all of the profits," said Diego.

"What profits? You don't mean them God people, do you?"

"Hey, what about my pet store?" said Jose.

"Boys, boys, I'll go to all o' your stores and spend lots o' money. Now how's that sound," said Louie.

"Say, you know what, Louie, its gettin' late out here," said Bill. "I think we best be leavin. Oh, wait…before I forget, what all happened to Anthony's son? You was sayin'?"

"He died in Korea and Ant'ny junior was his only kid."

"That's too bad."

"It took a while, but he finally found a way to deal with it. So now he has a new son. He's a happy man again."

***

One of the houses where Bill and Diego worked trimming the back yard and sweeping the front of the building belonged to a newly appointed assemblyman, James Richards. He lived in a brownstone in Park Slope, a twenty minute walk from Boerum Hill.

"You fellows did a nice job in the yard the last time you were here. When was that, Monday?"

"Yes sir," Diego said.

"Well...after you're done, I'd like for you both to take a look at my living room. I need to have it painted."

"We can do that for you, Mista Richards," said Bill. "It'd be our pleasure."

Two days later

Bill and Diego stepped back to admire their handiwork.

"Looks damn good, don' it?" said Bill.

"Sure does." Diego checked the clock. "It's nearly five o'clock. Mister Richards is going to be here any second, now."

No sooner did they start the cleanup, when in walked the assemblyman, and right on time. He was pleased with what he saw. On top of the twenty five dollars, he added another five and handed it to them.

"How about a soda, boys?"

"That is fine by me," said Bill.

"Thanks, Mr. Richards," said Diego.

"Say...I'll be needing help to clean up the leaves in the fall and someone to shovel snow. Can I count on the both of you?"

"Sho 'nough," said Bill.

"You know what, fellas? I noticed something about the both of you that I really like...your manners and show of respect. Now, I know where a southern gentleman like yourself gets it from, Bill, but it's both surprising and refreshing to see a young boy in the neighborhood speak so well for himself. What influenced you? I'm curious."

"My father, sir. Popi came from an upper middle class family in Puerto Rico. They had a lot of land wealth and a few businesses in San Juan."

"So, why didn't he stay there?"

"My father dropped out of college to join the army. He was very patriotic and wanted to do his part in winning the war. Roosevelt and General McArthur were his heroes. It was appreciation, I guess, a thank you of sorts for the success of his family, you might say."

"So, was he an officer in World War Two?"

"A sergeant. He got his leg blown off at Juno beach during the Normandy invasion. He lost a kidney and had some other internal wounds that I'm not too sure about."

"So he's a military type of disciplinarian?"

"To a point. Popi was actually easy going and soft spoken. He liked to say he was a man of values and of proud Spanish heritage and fine upbringing. He also liked to say, 'We come from a cultured background and I don't want you to ever forget that, son.'"

"You keep saying was. Isn't he still around?"

"Oh, no, sir. Popi died a couple of years ago. I guess those old war wounds finally caught up to him."

"My goodness! So what happened to all of that family wealth?"

"It's still there. His stepmother grabbed it years ago when my grandfather died. My father was still recuperating at Veteran's Hospital after the war when a letter from her attorney arrived. She had the legal rights to everything and used the excuse that my father abandoned the family so she could keep it all for herself. Popi often talked about taking her to court, but never seemed to find money or the energy to fight it."

"What about his education? Wasn't he able to get a good job?"

"He tried, but with so many soldiers coming back at the same time, he kept getting passed up because of his medical setbacks. He had only finished two years of college which wasn't enough for the teaching job he wanted. He ended up a clerk in a hotel."

"Where was that, where you live now?"

"No! Rochester…Upstate. That's where we lived until three years ago."

"I see, so…that's why you don't have a Brooklyn accent."

"Popi moved here to be close to Veterans' Hospital, near the army base."

"Right here in Brooklyn? Fort Hamilton, isn't it?"

"That's right, but he died anyway. I thought I'd never get over that. We were close."

"You're a stronger man than you think…and now you're taking care of your mother."

"I help out, and with the help of Mr. Jackson I bought my own school clothes."

"I'm glad to hear that, and that we'll be seeing more of one another."

"I hope so, Mr. Richards. If you ever need us, we're available, right Bill?"

Bill patted the boy's shoulder. "That's right. We is partners?"

"We sure are. Are you ready to slip me five, Mr. J?"

The two slapped palms, put their hands back to back and with the thumbs hooked together, used them like a hinge to flip their hands back around. They finished by sliding the palms across each other.

Chapter Four
P.S.6

Most days, Junior High School was a piece of cake. Diego found Hector in his homeroom, again. They sat together in the back row of the ninth grade class.

"My name is Mr. Bumblestein. I'm your substitute teacher for today and I'm not putting up with any of your nonsense. And that means you back there, mister! You, with the red plaid shirt! What's your name?"

"That's Hector," a freckle faced girl with red pig tails promptly volunteered.

"Hector, do you always come to class wearing your shirt outside your pants?"

"Yes, sir!"

"Don't get snippy with me. Go out in the hall right now and tuck that shirt back in."

"Yes sir, Mr. Bumblebean."

The class laughed.

"Bumblestein! Bumblestein! Do it now smart aleck. And what are you laughing at?" He said, pointing at Diego.

Sorry Mr. Bumblebee.

"Nothing, Mr. Bumblestein, sir."

"So you thought that was funny, too? Sit back down!"

After ten minutes, the teacher opened the door to the hall and looked both ways for Hector. The student was gone.

"Fine! When he gets back, I'll have a talk with him. The rest of you vegetables, write an essay on the school's dress code. And I want at least three long paragraphs."

"Can I write it in Spanish?" a boy by the window asked.

"No, lame brain. English! And no more talking!"

"I was only asking."

"Don't ask! Just do! Get busy...all of you!"

Hector returned and after a short briefing in the hall on the school's dress code, he was allowed to return to his seat next to Diego where he was given instructions for the essay.

The room, quiet for about twenty long minutes, began to stir with the taps of carefully placed pens as one by one they were each left dormant above finished essays waiting to be picked up.

"You! Collect every one of these and bring them up to the front."

The same girl who ratted out Hector, collected the paper work and handed them over.

Shuffling through them quickly, the teacher said, "None of these are any good. Do you know what I think of your fine grammar?"

Rip! Every last essay was torn to pieces and dropped into the waste basket.

"I'm going to write a few rules on the blackboard and I want everyone to copy them."

Mr. Bumblestein turned his back to the class and started to write---and with quite an artistic penmanship:

We must always adhere to the rules set forth by the school.

We must never wear jeans, shorts, baseball caps...

Sitting in a row directly in front of Diego and Hector, Willy Goodwin leaned over and whispered to TJ, "Yeah, that's right...I still have them."

Willy slunk low in his chair and stretched to retrieve three darts out of a plain, denim school bag.

"Let me do it," TJ whispered.

"No, their mine, I'll do it."

Bumblestein, still writing on the blackboard, barked, "What are you two jabbering about back there? Be quiet and wait until I'm finished."

THWACK...THWACK...THWACK

Bumblestein's head whipped around. "What the devil just happened? "Who threw those?"

Diego could not believe what he just saw. Willie Goodwin threw three darts at the cork board and only a couple of feet away from the teacher. He immediately held his head between his two hands in disbelief.

No one else in class, other than Hector and TJ, had seen who had actually thrown the darts. The only movement some of them did see was Diego's hands when he lowered them to his lap.

No one answered. The smirks and muffled giggling enraged the teacher, and his reddening face only encouraged them more. He banged on his desk.

"Okay, we'll play that game. You! Yes, you! I want you to pass around these strips of paper to everyone in this class. Now, I'm sure at least some of you here know who threw those darts. You don't have to sign your name. All I want you to do is write down the party or parties involved. Go ahead, pass them around."

The girl with pigtails put a slip of paper on each desk. When the class finished scribbling names, she collected the folded notes and brought them to the front.

"So...you think you're all so smart? Well, we'll see about that. Shall I read these to you? Never mind! The first one says...I do not know, I did not see nothing."

(Laughter)

"Whoever wrote that, there are never two no's in a sentence and you have three. Here's the next one...Elmer Fudd! Humph!"

(More laughter)

"Shh! Aha! Here! Diego Rivera! Now where getting someplace. What else is in here? Let's see." Mr. Bumblestein mumbled the rest of the names to himself, "The Long Ranger, Daffy Duck, The President, Howdy Doody. Hah!" He loudly exclaimed. "Another Diego!"

"Oooo!" The class responded.

Diego closed his eyes and retreated into quiet thought.

So, now you think it was me, right Mr. Bumblebee? And who do you think you are coming into my classroom to harass me and my fellow students?

Now...you do know what I'm going to have to do to you, don't you, Mr. Bumblebee? Yes, that's right, I'm going to have to get that nasty old broom out of the closet and whack you with it until all of those righteous wings come off. But do you also know what I'm doing to you after that? I'm going to crush you under my right shoe like the...bug...you... are. Got that, Bumbles? SMACK! SMACK! SMACK!

Bumblestein read another slip of paper. "Hmm, what's this? You! Very Funny, who wrote that? Hm...Space men...Froggy." *Damn stupid kids.* "Okay... here's Diego Rivera again."

Diego eyed the teacher with contempt. Sure, and that just fills you with glee, doesn't it Mr. Bumblebee. It just tickles...you...to...death to be so sure it was me.

"That's three for Diego Rivera and I don't see anyone else's name on any of these."

Of course not, Mr. Bumbles. They're all afraid of you and now they're your friends.

"Well! I think we have our little dart thrower. Come up to the front, right now, Mr. Rivera."

"But, Mr. Bumbles…it wasn't me!"

By now the kids were hysterical.

"Oh, I'm sorry. I meant, Bumblebee. No! I mean, Mr. Bumblestein, sir. It really wasn't me."

"If you kids don't stop laughing, I'll make every one of you stay after school…and I mean it."

"He didn't do it," said Hector.

"And why should I believe you, smart aleck? All right, Diego, If it wasn't you, then who was it?"

"I don't know, sir. I wasn't looking."

"Then how do you explain why three students said it was you? Now come up here to the front like I said."

Diego gave a mad face to Willie. He wasn't a snitch, but if he got the chance, he was going to get even outside after three.

Mr. Bumblestein said, "You're going with me to the principal's office right after class, Mister. You thought you were pulling the wool over my eyes, didn't you?"

Diego never got the chance to meet anybody after three. Instead, he landed in the lunch room with two hours detention. He felt miserable.

A letter arrived by mail a few days later. Diego wasn't home when it got there and he hadn't said anything to his mother about the incident. She couldn't read English very well anyway. Perhaps he could bluff his way through this one, he had thought. What she didn't know wouldn't hurt her.

"Karen read these papers to me today and I don't like it, Mr. Diego Rivera."

Saying his full name was always a bad sign, especially when she rolled the r's with her tongue.

"Mom, it really wasn't me. I got blamed for it, but nobody really saw what happened."

"So why don't you tell me these things when they happen instead of waiting for me to get a letter from school?"

"I thought you might not get a letter. Hector was sitting right there. He knows it wasn't me."

"So now you want Hector to lie for you?"

"I'm not lying, Mom. Oh, what's the use? You're not going to believe me anyway."

"Karen told me that I have to see the principal."

"I'm sorry, Mom."

"Sorry? Sorry? It's too late for being sorry. You know I can't walk with this hip."

"I know, but it wasn't me. It really wasn't."

"I want to believe you, but even if it wasn't you, Diego, the teacher believed it was you."

Next Day; Principal's Office

"Come in! Have a seat right there, Mr. Rivera. And who is that with you?"

"This is Mr. Jackson, Mr. Ratzfarb. He's a family friend. My mother couldn't come. She has a bad hip and can't walk very far."

"That's perfectly fine. Do you know what this is all about, Mr. Jackson?"

"I gots the gist of it, suh. But you see, Diego is a good boy. I knows him for quite some time now and…"

"Well, Mr. Jackson, you know this boy for quite some time, but I guess you don't really know him very well after all, do you? He put one of my teachers in danger with these darts?"

The principal tapped hard on the desk with a forefinger. "These darts! These darts right here!"

"Suh…alls ah knows is that he ain't done nothin' of the kind in all the time that I knows him. We been a workin' all summer long togetha, an' I can tell you, Mista Principal, suh, if he says he ain't done did it, then that be the truth. Please, suh, he ain't never even did hissalf nothin' in the fust place."

"You got a three day suspension, Mr. Rivera, and that's the end of it. You can go now."

"Yes, sir."

Diego trailed behind Bill's slow steps; the elderly man's head slunk between his shoulders as he exited through the door.

Out in the hall, Bill fumed, "That man ain't heard nothin' ah said. If ah could put his dot sized brain in a gnat's butt, I betcha that bug would fly backwards."

In the ensuing silence of his office, Mr. Ratzfarb sat and stared at the closed door. He continued to tap on the desk with the end of a pencil for a while…a long while. Something about this whole thing bothered him. If he could only put his finger on it. More tapping. Finally, that "something" sparked his memory.

"Betty Ann!"

His secretary cracked the door open. "Yes, Mr. Ratzfarb?"

"You remember something last year about darts being thrown in the school yard…or…I don't know, I can't remember exactly who it was or where, but there was an incident about darts? Do you remember that?"

"That was in the lunch room. That Willie kid… um…Willie Goodwin."

"That's right…Goodwin! Is he in Diego's class this year?"

"I believe so. Do you want me to pull his file?"

"No, don't bother. It's all settled for now and I really don't have time to pursue any of it. Never mind. Thanks anyway."

Aside from the incident, Diego did very well in school. He was especially good at math, inherited from his mother he had always thought. She was good at calculations---did it all in her head.

School Assembly

It was halfway through the school year and time to give out awards. The assembly room was now full with every seat taken and many of the parents left standing along the back wall.

"It's too bad Mom couldn't come. I know she really wanted to."

Beulah patted Diego on the knee. "She proud a ya'll anyways, son. She woulda been here if it weren't for no hip a hurtin' her so. And ya'll doin' all o' this here learnin' all by yo-self? It jus' be makin' us so proud."

After the Pledge of Allegiance and God Bless America were sung by all, along with the accompaniment of the school band, and more than a few out of key voices with no clue as to the lyrics, a few speeches were made. A poem was recited on stage by a student and then a piano rendition of "Flight of the Bumblebee", (No pun intended…okay, so it was) followed by a medley of Christmas songs sung by the Ninth Grade Chorus.

Mr. Ratzfarb, awards in hand, once again graced the stage with his pomp-ass presence. "I would now like to express my deepest gratitude and appreciation for…"

"You know somethin', Beulah?"

"What's that, Mista Jackson?"

"I'd like to kick that man so high, birds would build a nest in his ears before he hit the ground."

"Now, you know that ain't polite like."

"Well, I ain't lookin' to be polite like, no-how."

Beulah took the moment to ask Diego something. "Do you thank ya'll might git one of those awards today, Diega?"

"I was hoping I would. I got straight A's. Remember the report cards I showed you?"

"I sho do, and we so proud a ya'll, too."

("And for perfect attendance...")

"I got an A+ for my book report, so...we'll see, but there's a lot of smart kids out here, and besides, I don't think Mr. Ratzfarb really likes me."

"Aw, shush," said Bill. "He ain't gonna pay that dart thang no never mind. His pea brain done forgot it already. Don't you fret none."

("Now, in science we have...")

"It don't matter if'n you don't get nothin'" Diega," said Beulah, with another reassuring tap on the knee. "We gonna give you our own award, ain't we, Mr. Jackson?"

"We sho is. We gots somethin' await'n in the wings. Ya'll sit tight, son."

Both Beulah's and the principal's words melded into the background as Diego transcended to an ancient gladiator's ring. There, he stood steadfast with a Roman pugio in his grip. Ratzfarbius stabbed at him with his sword and missed, which Diego kicked out of his hand, casting the weapon to the side. He reached for his opponent's bronze, frowning face mask and grabbed it underneath the jaw. With the good hold he had, he threw Ratzfarbius viciously to the ground. He stepped on his hasta sword, still in its sheath, squatted over him and pointed the pugio at his throat.

As a cloud of sunlit dust settled around them, Diego cocked his head to the side to find Tiberius, sitting in his gilded cubicle high above the horde of cheering spectators. Beneath a blue and unhampered sky, the Emperor leapt from his throne and in response to the jeering crowd, his thumb, like theirs, thrust suddenly downward.

"Spare me, oh master Diego," Ratzfarbius pleaded. "I faulted you and now I feel nothing but shame. Whilst thou ever forgive me?"

Another look at the Emperor and the decision was set. Diego raised the pugio high and…

("…and for excellence in Math, Diego Rivera. Diego, come up and receive your award.")

"You sees! I told you so! Now git on up there and see us proud." Bill winked at Beulah and turned to watch the boy as he headed down the aisle.

The grin on Diego's face stretched as pats on the back followed him to the end of the row. He trotted up to the stage and quickly made his way to the podium. "Hello Mr. Ratzfarb."

The principal covered the mike and softly spoke in a half whisper. "You did really well for yourself this semester. We're pushing you up a grade. That means you will be starting your junior year in high school next September. I'll talk to you about that later. Right now I have to say something to the good folks out there…so straighten up.

"Eh, ehem…"

Squeel! Sqreeeech! Tap! Tap! Tap!

"I'd like to say to everyone sitting in this audience that even a once troubled student like Diego Rivera can benefit from the expertise of a well trained staff that has…

"…and so we here at P.S. 6 have strived to improve…

"…and through diligent follow up and a hard line, turned a failing student around…

"…and finally, Mr. Rivera, thank you so much for all of your hard work. Here's your award."

(Handshake)

"You may sit down." The principal turned back to the audience. "Let's all give a wonderful hand for Diego Rivera. And thank you everyone for coming today to a most fruitful and produ…"

Bill grimaced. "That man near broke his arm pattin' himself on the back."

***

(KNOCK…KNOCK…KNOCK)
Ana opened the door.

"Mrs. Rivera?" Asked a tall, well-dressed man in a dark suit and striped tie.

"Si?"

"Hello, my name is James Richards. I'm the district Assemblyman. I have something to ask you that concerns your son."

"Of course! Please come in. Have a seat."

Diego stood up from the couch, surprised to see the assemblyman standing there.

"Actually," Mr. Richards began, "I'm in the middle of a few errands and I only had a moment to stop by to ask you something. I'm taking a couple of the kids from the Colony House to the Museum of Natural History in the city tomorrow. If you would like to go, Diego, you're more than welcomed to come along."

Diego's face brightened. "Gee, Mom…can I?"

Ana nodded. "Should he pack a lunch?"

"That won't be necessary. I'm treating them all to pizza afterwards."

"Can Hector go, Mr. Richards?" Diego asked.

"Absolutely! One more won't make a difference. Go ahead and ask him. Either way, meet us at the Colony House before twelve tomorrow afternoon."

"Is that enough time? Why so late?" Ana asked.

"Well, you know how kids are, they get bored fairly quickly. Most of them only want to see dinosaurs. After that they get a little rambunctious."

"What time are you planning to get back?"

"Around six or seven. I'll make sure it's not too late."

Chapter Five
Hell's Kitchen

Later that evening

Barnes returned tired from work---too many kids in the theatre today---up and down, up and down. It seemed all he did the entire shift was do nothing but go up and down the aisles chasing the misbehaved kids that were throwing popcorn off the balcony, peeing from their seats, or groping one another in the back row. He must have tossed out at least a half a dozen of them.

He relaxed on the front stoop sipping a beer. Although late, he couldn't sleep---perhaps in an hour or so. He needed to unwind a bit first.

From where he was sitting he could see into Ana's window, the red floral, plastic curtain spread wide and revealing. Now and then he caught a full view of her limping around in her panties and bra.

Nice legs! Not bad for a crippled broad. I wouldn't mind doin' her. Hell, I might just knock on her door in the morning. Crap! Tomorrow's Saturday. The kid's home. Damn!

Wait a minute…they're off until after New Year's. It's the holidays. Well, that sucks!

Joe continued to stare through the window.

Someday I'm gonna do it. I'm gonna do her…I really am.

He stood straight and gulped down what was left inside the bottle. After double checking that no one would see, he edged closer to the window.

Look at that! Twelve thirty at night and that stupid kid's watchin' Flash Gordon. When the hell does he go to bed?

He watched as Ana stepped in front of the sink. He couldn't keep his eyes off her.

Saturday Afternoon 1:40 P.M.

Back on the stoop from Herzog's, Joe finished an egg on a roll and sipped black coffee from a paper cup. He said nothing to Karen's little girls, all bundled up as they ran by and clambered down the front steps and then skipped to the other side of the street. There, they met another girl where they started to play hop scotch on the sidewalk.

The outside door creaked open. Barnes faced it and was pleasantly surprised.

"What brings you out on a chilly day like this?"

Ana smiled gently and in a soft voice, said, "I'm looking for the girls to go to the store for me. Aren't you going to work today, Joe?"

"Yeah, two o'clock. Where's your son?"

"He went to the museum with some people from the colony house. They just left."

"Oh! Won't be back for a while, huh?"

"No! Tonight…six or seven, something like that."

"Tonight, huh?" Barnes focused on her perfectly round ass as she reentered the building.

Crap! And I gotta go to work in 35 minutes. Saturdays suck. Same old crap, damn unruly fuckin'…

Wait a sec. Yeah…that's what I'll do. I'll go in to work and wait for the feature film to start. I'll show myself in the aisles and shine my flash light in a few faces. Yeah… that's it, let 'em know I'm there. After that, I'll pass by the ticket booth, give the old hag a wave and check the bathroom real quick. That way, it'll look like I'm doing my job. I can slip out the back stock room unnoticed and catch the bus. I'll probably get back here by three thirty, give or take, do what I want to do to her, then take care of things so she can't rat me out. I should be back at work before the second feature starts. Ha! I'll have a good alibi. Nobody will even know I was gone.

2:27 *P.M.* The Brooklyn Fox Theatre

Barnes made a final pass up the aisles. By the time the coming attractions finished in a few more minutes he would have a head start on the first movie. He checked that Edith, the old spinster behind the ticket window saw him walk by, nodded and headed for the concession stand. There, he dilly dallied around a bit before moving on to the men's room.

It was empty when he went in. Normally he would have checked the booths, pulling each of the doors wide open as he went by. It was something he always did. Not that he cared if anyone was actually taking a dump, but to see if maybe a couple of guys were in there doing something they shouldn't be doing. That's when he'd nail them. Extortion was profitable. Catching lovers in the act put money in his pockets. Either that or he'd threaten to turn them over to the cops, or at the least, harass the shit out of them. But not now! There was no time for that. He was impatient to get back to Dean Street.

Joe looked up toward the bathroom door as it suddenly opened, followed by a familiar, 'though unwelcomed voice.

"Well looky, looky over heah who we all found in da baretroom. Guess who-id-is, Tommy? Dear old Mista Joe, da wiggly woim, Barnes."

Shit! …"Er…uh…hi Fast Eddie. So how's things going?"

Fast Eddie was the type of guy that did everything slow. He even talked slow, hence the spoof on the name play. Burdened with a speech impediment from a deformed palate, he sounded like a cross between Sach from the Bowery Boys and Elmer Fudd. Along with a strong West Side accent, he at times was hard to understand, even by acquaintances from his own neighborhood. Frail in stature, it only added to his insecurities, which he made up for with the tough guy persona.

Under an open coat he wore a size 38, white dress shirt pressed to a T with the collar up in back. Three top buttons were left open to show off the thick, curly hairs of his bony chest. Black, greasy hair, loaded down with copious amounts of Brill Cream, lay flat and slicked down at the sides. Above his forehead, a skillfully sculptured pompadour curls like a high wave approaching a sandy beach.

With a matter of fact tone in his voice, and chewing a fat wad of gum that he liked to snap as he spoke, he said, "Tings ain't so good Barnes." *(Snap!)* "At least not for you, dat is." (Pop!) "There's a little matta of some money you owes somebody, rememba? Or dids ya forget? Now I knows it's been awhile, so let me refresh your memory. Does ten thousan' clams soun' familia?"

"I ain't got it, Eddie. I really don't. And how the hell did you find me, anyway?"

"Da want ads, ya meat head." *(Snap)* "Howdya tink we found ya?" *(Snap… Pop)* "We had our boys all over the city lookin' for ya, dat's how." *(Pop)*

"I'm really broke, Eddie. I don't have it! Honest! Look at my face, would I lie to you? Why, I'm so honest, I wouldn't even keep a wallet if I found one in the street…you know?

"And you know what else? I don't even have a gun anymore, you know? Somebody robbed my room and took it, I tell you. They even took my week's pay lying on the nightstand. And a while back, some bum hit me in the back of the head on the way home. I had amnesia for months, you know? I'd pay you if I had the money, honest I woul...."

Half interested, Fast Eddie finished blowing an expanding pink bubble while listening to Joe's B-S. Sucking it back in, he said, "Aw...alladat's too bad, Barnes. Hey Tommy!" (*Snap!*) "Look at da cry baby. He ain't got it, he says."

Tommy looked over at Barnes from watching the door with a half smoked Pall Malls between his lips. Hanging off the end were ashes as long as the cigarette. "Agh...fuck it Eddie, do'm and let's get da fuck outta here. I wanna get a coupla hot dawgs. I'm starvin'."

Barnes' face wrinkled as he pleaded. "Come on, man. You don't have to do this. Give me a little time."

"A little time, da Barnes says. You must be outta your chimney, Santy Claus?" (*Snap*) "Hey, Tommy! Stay by dat daw and make sure nobody comes in."

Tommy stared back with raised brows as though his head emptied of all brain matter. "What if somebody taps on the door, whaddo I do, Eddie?"

"Sings happy boitday to 'em. Whaddya askin' me fa, ya peanut bwittle bwain? Can't ya tink fa yaself? Just tell 'em we're moppin' da floor, dimwit." He spit the gum out. "Now get over dere, Barnes, you're really pissin' me off and dat ain't no good, see? Ova dere in da corna...nice 'n' slow."

"What are you gonna do, Eddie?"

"You'll see. Just get over dere and shet yer mout'."

"Don't shoot, Eddie. I'll do anything."

"Listen to da creep. Don't shoot! Don't shoot! Ya shoulda taudadat befaw?"

"Waste'm Eddie. Before somebody comes," said Tommy. "Give'm both barrels."

"Boat Barrels? Dis is a 45, woach bwain, Tommy. It ain't got but one barrel. You been watchin' too many of doze cops and robba shows what's in da movies. Now watch da daw like I tol' ya." He turned to face Joe. "Look Barnes...ya needs to listen up, dickhead."

"Hey, come on, Eddie, I'll do whatever you want."

"Agh...shaddap ya scwew ball. Shoulda toudadat when ya had da chance. Now bend over and smile for da cam'ra."

"Please, I'll do anything."

"Anyting he says. He'll do anyting, Tommy. I dunno, should we listen to him?"

"Help me, Tommy! Tell him not to shoot! Tell him, Tommy! You and me...we go way back. We were partners, remember? Tell him!"

Tommy wedged his foot against the bottom of the door and returned a look of distain. "Shoot da leach suckin' piece o' shit, Eddie. Whaddya waitin' for?"

"Shut up, Tommy. You ain't da boss. Ay, Barnes! Hurry up and bend over and touch yer toes so we can get da hell outa heah, huh? Hey, look, I'll be real quick like. Ya won't even feels a ting. I promise."

"I said I'll do anything and I meant it? Just ask me, Eddie? Anything!"

"Whad a freakin' looza. You're a freakin' sap, Barnes, ya know dat? So you'll do anyting, huh? Okay...okay, look...don't shit your diapers ya little cry baby. So ya wants a break den, duz ya?"

"Just this one time, Eddie. I'll...I'll rob a store or something...or a bank. Whatever you ask."

"Stop yer squawkin,' ya two timin' looza. And don't tell me howda run my damn business. I'll tell you! You don't tell me!"

(Knock...Knock)

"See who it is, pencil head!"

Tommy cracked the door and took a peek. "It's only a coupla kids."

"Tell 'em to go pee in dere pants somewheah else. Nah! Neva mind! Jess' tell 'em real sweet like to come back in ten minutes...or sump'm like dat."

Tommy opened the door and gave the boys a pleasant smile. "Hi kids...go away or I'm gonna slap dem fuckin' buck teets outa your mouts!" He slammed the door. "They said okay, Eddie!"

"Fine! So dis is what youz's gonna do for us, ya big palooka. You're gonna bumps off Sally Boy whats hangs out on Mulberry, down in little Italy for us... ya gots dat?"

"Sally Boy! Yeah Eddie, I got it. I'll bump him off for you."

"You bet your friggin' bottom dolla ya will, ya big piece a woach manewa."

"Tommy...take out dat red, fancy switchblade whats ya bought at da dime store. Da one from Forty Second Stweet."

"I thought we had a deal, Eddie?"

"We does, mista looza, Barnes, da idiot wid potato fa bwains, only we gotta sign some legal papers foist. Cut'm Tommy!"

Barnes' face twisted in pain. "Ow! …What the hell…damn! I said I'd do it, didn't I?"

Tommy pulled the knife out of the back of Joe's leg, making him fall to his knees.

"Damn, that hurt!" Joe cried.

"Well, give the scolla a friggin' diploma. No kiddin' it hoit, Dick Tracy. Its supposta, ya big shit! Hey! Talking 'bout shit, did you jest crap your pants?"

"I…I think I did," Joe shrieked, looking down and feeling his wet backside.

Eddie frowned with disgust. "Holy Toledo! You smell like a friggin' slime bag! Why you're nuttin' but a low lyin', bottom o' da sewa, shit suckin' slug. An' a slug wit' no balls, no less. "Give'm anudda paper ta sign soze we can catch'm if he tries to run away."

"Ow!" Joe cried.

Wiping the blade off on Joe's pants, Tommy folded it up and put it back in his pocket.

"Where's da back daw to dis place?" Fast Eddie asked.

"Out there to the left. Just don't stab me no more."

Eddie stepped away from him. Clean dat shit up and wrap da wound wit turly paper. You're comin' wid us."

5:30 P.M.
514 West 48th Street Manhattan

Mickey Spillane's apartment---a real dive of a hellhole, in a dump of a neighborhood. It wasn't always that way, though. Back during the day of the Dutch, the Great Kills, a confluence of three streams, joined close to here near what is now 10th Avenue and 40th Street. A small hamlet developed where carriages were built adjacent to the farm of Andreas Hopper. His land stretched from Sixth Avenue to the East River and from 48th to 59th.

Beginning in 1849, the New York to Poughkeepsie Steam Railroad transformed the area into tanneries and warehouses. Then came the potato famine and the subsequent waves of Irish immigrants. Their families were sprawled all along the Hudson River in shanty towns. Gangs soon took over and prospered and with the ensuing congestion, tenements rose up in Hell's Kitchen. During the prohibition that followed, the gangs readily fattened their wallets.

Owney Madden and his Gopher Gang took over after the prohibition, relying instead on gambling, loan sharking, union shake-downs, prostitution and other lucrative ventures. But he was gone from the Kitchen now, and Mickey Spillane owns all of it, despite the mafia's control of the rest of the city. This was now Spillane's exclusive stronghold and he aggressively protected it. Even the best of the mafia's henchmen knew to keep their distance.

"Go on upsteahs, Barnes," Fast Eddie prodded.

Barnes took a deep breath, but his heart was racing inside like a taxi late for a VIP flight at Idlewild. He felt so lousy he wanted to puke. He entered the apartment and meekly waved at the staring figure behind the large desk.

"Hi boss. You know what, I'm really sorry about the loan. It's all a misunderstanding, you know? You see...I was only in Brooklyn to, eh...well, you know, I had to go to a funeral, and then I was offered a job, and then one thing lead to another, my mother got sick, and then, you know, I got mugged in the subway and got my ass kicked in pretty bad, had a few teeth knocked out and after that I got hit by a bus and had to walk with crutches and..."

"Shut the fuck up Barnes, will ya?" said Mickey Spillane. "I don't wanna hear any more of your bullshit. And stop bleedin' all over my floor. By the way, how come you smell like shit?"

"Long story, Boss," said Fast Eddie.

"Somebody get'm a rag. Did any of you tell Barnes what I wannid him to do?"

"Yeah, sure Boss, I tol'm. He already knows," Fast Eddie said.

"Good! Good! Then you know...right Barnes?"

"Yeah, sure, Boss...no problem...Sally Boy, right?"

"That's right...tonight at seven o fuckin' clock. Right after he eats his spaghetti 'n' meatballs. I want that guy dead! Big Jimmy, give this whimp a Luger with two in the chamber."

From an overstuffed chair in the corner, Big Jimmy, "The Geek" Maguire, who originally hailed from Akron, Ohio, grunted as he got all 6' foot 6" and 350 pounds of himself to his feet to empty the Luger, leaving two bullets in the gun.

Mickey Spillane pointed his finger at Joe. "Take this gun and no funny business or the boys'll put some holes in ya where you're not supposed to have no holes."

Jimmy the Geek slapped the gun into Joe's hand, sunk back into an easy chair, lit a cigar and farted, "Sorry Boss, too much cabbage."

By now, Joe was sweating his own set of bullets. "After this, we're even right? I don't owe you a thing, right?"

"If you're talkin' 'bout the ten thousand you owe me, I'll think about it."

"But Mickey, you said all I have to do is bump off Sally Boy in Little Italy?"

"Who said that wuz all?" Mickey Spillane feigned looking behind himself. He checked underneath the desk and then looked around the room. "I neva said nuttin' like that. Was it you, Big Jimmy?"

Maguire frowned. His voice, fully basso and resonant, shook the floor boards like a jack hammer. "I didn't say anything like that."

"Did you, Fast Eddie?"

"Nope! I ain't said nuttin' like dat, needa."

"What about you Tommy? Yo, Tommy, wake up!"

Tommy opened his eyes and rubbed them. "Huh? What?"

"Nah, neva mind! Ya see, Barnes, you ain't heard it from none of us, but I'll tells ya what…if it goes off wid ouda a hitch, I might just maybe give you a free ride."

"What…what exactly do you mean by a free ride, Mickey?"

"Now, waddya tink It means, lunkhead. A free ride! A…free…ef'en, fuckin' ride. That's all! What! You also gotta know where the ride's goin'?"

"Yeah, you'll see," Tommy snickered.

"What's he mean by, I'll see?" Joe asked, with a worried look.

Spillane shook his head. "Why can't ya shet your mout', Tommy. You're gonna scare the bajeezes outa da guy. Big Jimmy, escort this…this Barnes to the backroom until six."

Joe stopped in the hallway, looked back at Spillane and with a forced smile, gently asked, "Can somebody order a pizza, Mickey? I'm a little hungry?"

"Eh…yeah, sure…why not. Call Angelo's and order a coupla pizzas. And get some sodas. And yo…hey Barnes!"

"Yeah, Boss?"

"Wash dem shitty underwears of yaws and take a freakin' shower. You smell like my Aunt Tilly's asshole."

Fast Eddie laughed at that. "What was ya doin' down dere smellin' your Aunt Tilly's butt hole, for?"

"You see me laughin', Eddie?"

"Sorry, Boss."

7:12 P.M.

The ride downtown went slow, due to heavy traffic. A few blocks into Grand Street, Jimmy the Geek turned the fire engine red, '59 "Cat Eyes", Impala, in toward the curb and parked in front of a hydrant. He stepped out, slammed the door and circled around to the other side.

"Get the fuck out!"

Barnes had been shaking the whole way down Broadway. It's not that he didn't want to kill anybody. He had done that plenty of times. It was the stress of getting caught out in the open, and the last thing he wanted was another stint in the slammer; and a life sentence at that.

It was still light out and a lot of people were around. He felt under his jacket for the Luger and left it where it was, stuffed behind his belt. Limping ahead, he put his hands in his pockets and kept his head down.

"Remember, Barnes, I'll be right behind you," said the Geek.

While the two continued toward the restaurant, Tommy got out, walked to the back of the car and clipped a couple of bogus Jersey plates over the New York ones. He returned to the driver's seat and slid behind the steering wheel with Fast Eddie taking the back seat right behind him.

Tommy waited for the last of a string of cars to ride past and roll on ahead before muscling the steering wheel left. The red beast edged away from the curb and crept slowly behind Big Jimmy, who was on the sidewalk just a few feet behind Barnes. They were nearing the cross street of Mulberry and would soon cross over to Carmine's restaurant on the far corner.

Inside the Chevy, Tommy said, "Wit' alla dese people around, the coppers are gonna get the goods on Barnes."

"Yeah," said Fast Eddie, "dey'll figga it's him, but when dey get 'm in da back room, chicken snitch is gonna spill all a da beans 'bout what he knows aboud us."

"He'll squeal like da pig he is, dat's for sure."

Sally Boy was where he always was after seven, sitting at a table by the front window, pushing the last of a pile of spaghetti onto a fork with a stubby forefinger. Next to that, a fat cannoli sat on a flowered cake dish alongside a cup of cappuccino mixed with a double shot of anisette.

(BLAM…BLAM)

People everywhere ran up and down the street in panic. Some took refuge in doorways while others ducked behind cars.

Fast Eddie shouted at the driver. "Step on it Tommy. Get up there an' pick 'em up."

Jimmy the Geek jumped into the front seat, rocking the car like a capsizing row boat.

Shots returned from deep inside the restaurant, with Joe slamming the front door wide open and running for his life across the sidewalk.

Tommy lunged the car forward another few yards and jammed on the brakes in front of Barnes.

"Get in, fuck head!" Eddie yelled, while holding the back door wide open.

Barnes jumped in with the door banging shut behind him from the forward momentum of Tommy flooring the gas guzzling 348 for all it was worth.

"Give me the gun, Barnes," ordered Big Jimmy, reaching over the back seat.

Eddie shouted to Tommy. "Shoot down toid avenew and takes Houston straight to da East Riva, den jumps on da highway!"

"Which way do I go from there?" said Tommy.

"Which way? Da way we's always goes! Uptown, bwittle bwain! Jeesh!"

The four settled in and after turning onto Houston, they stopped for a light at Avenue B. Fast Eddie, pointing to a gas station across the street, said, "Hey, ya knows what? We gotta make room for, er, ah…whats's name?"

"Who," Tommy asked? "We ain't gotta get nobody."

"Big Jimmy nudged Tommy in the leg with his foot while winking his right eye a couple of times. "Yeah…you know!" *(Wink…wink)* "Ol' Smiley Smitty? You remember him?" He faced the back seat and subtly returned Fast Eddie's slow head nod.

"Smitty who?" Tommy asked, still dumbfounded."

Eddie hit the back of Tommy's seat, "Jeesh, don't you know nuttin', Tommy? Smit! Ol' Smiley Smit Wesson? Now do you rememba?"

"Oh...oh yeah, dat Smiley Smit', I remember. Yeah, we gotta pick'm up for the last show, in...er...ah..."

The Geek smirked and loudly bassooned, "Central Park, pimple brain! Where did you think we were going? Pull behind the gas station over there and shut the lights off so I can sit in the back with our dear ol' pal, Joe Barnes."

"Yeah, soze we's can empty the front seat for Smiley Smitty, right, Big Jimmy?" Tommy winked back at the Geek with his right eye---the wrong eye. Luckily, Barnes hadn't noticed."

"Get out there and change the plate, Turd Ball," Jimmy ordered. "And keep your mouth shut for the rest of the trip."

Deep in thought, Joe had paid them, nor anything else they were saying any mind. He hadn't heard a thing.

I could have been back there finishing up with that spic broad by now. I could have had her and bumped her off. Instead, I'm stuck with these three arguing low lifes who aren't even worthy of licking the dirt from under my shoes.

As soon as I get to Brooklyn, I ain't waitin' for a good tip no more. I gotta bet the whole thing right away, before these loonies realize I still have the money. The next horse I pick with decent odds, I'm gonna bet the whole thing. All of it. Whatever I get, I get. Then I'm takin' the winnings and high tailing it back to Hicksville. Screw these guys. They ain't never gonna see the likes of me again. If I could, I'd first put a bullet into Fast Eddie's nickel sized brain, that fuckin' idiot. He had to go and find me, that piece of sh..."

Tommy got out, unclipped the Jersey plates, opened the trunk and threw them inside. As soon as he got behind the wheel, Jimmy the Geek was already in the rear seat with Barnes squeezed in the middle.

Up the FDR they went, nice and easy so as not to draw any attention. Off at 72nd, they crossed 5th Avenue and drove into Central Park where they took the park drive north to the boathouse. It was closed this time of day and vacant. Already, it was nearly dark out and the park the last place anybody would want to be.

"What are we doing here?" Joe asked, a lump in his throat.

"Don't you rememba? We gotta wait for ol' Smiley Smitty, that's all," Tommy said, with a giggle. "Yup...he'll get here when it gets a little darka, right, Big Jimmy?"

"Idiot!" Jimmy mumbled. He leaned against the door, turned his fat face amicably toward Joe and laid his heavy arm across his shoulders. While he talked, he kept patting him on the back. "You did a nice job back there, Barnes. Ain't that right, boys?"

"That's right...real good job," said Tommy.

"I couldena done it betta myself," Fast Eddie agreed. "Do ya tink dat Smitty guy's gonna' show up pretty soon?"

Jimmy looked at his watch...7:48. "Yeah, real soon! So Barnes...what do we do with you now, I mean...you being all paid up and all?"

"Me? Do with me? What do you mean?"

Outwardly, Barnes appeared as calm as a Times Square hooker counting a good days take. Inside, the fear searing through him felt like rotten peperoni belching up his esophagus. He'd been in situations like this before, except that in those situations he was on the giving end.

Big Jimmy said, "Well, I kinda thought you might be up for a promotion?"

"Really? Oh hell...I can do anything."

"I can vouch for dat anyting stuff," said Fast Eddie. "He'll definitely do anyting."

"Yeah, I can vouch for him, too," said Tommy, snickering.

"Gee! I wonder what kind of job we can give to the Barnes here to show our 'preciation," said the Geek.

"We could put'm in da warehouse," said Tommy. "You know...put 'm in charge of the chains and cement blocks...tee hee."

"Hey! Fuck you, Tommy," Joe barked. "What the hell is he talkin' about?"

"No! Fuck you, Barnes!" said Jimmy, taking his arm off his shoulder. "In fact, I think I see old Smitty Wesson coming this way right now."

"Wh...where? I don't see nobody," Joe nervously turned to look through each and every window.

"Oh, sure! He's right here!" The Geek leaned over the front seat and opened the glove box. He grabbed a nickel plated revolver lying inside and sat back with it, a Smith & Wesson 38, 1956 Model 10 with an optional six inch barrel. Attached to it, was a blue-steel silencer.

"Mr. Barnes, I want you to meet Mr. Smith and Wesson."

"Say, what gives? What the hell are you planning to do with that?" Barnes shouted in panic.

Jimmy Maguire didn't give him the courtesy of an answer. Instead, he spun the chamber around a few times with slow methodical movements to recheck that it was fully loaded. He then wrenched the silencer tight. "Take this slab of chicken crap behind the boathouse!"

"Wait! No, please! Don't do this!" Joe screamed.

Both Eddie and Tommy grabbed him by the ankles and dragged him out of the back, with Joe clawing at the seat fabric, screaming for his life.

On the other side of the car, The Geek squeezed his huge frame out and with his usual long strides, easily caught up. He grabbed Joe tightly by the scruff of the neck and forced him to walk faster. "Right over there. That'll do. Now… what happened to the money, Barnes?"

"The horses, Mr. Jimmy," Barnes hysterically blurted out loud. "Spillane knows I have a bad habit. I lost the whole thing on a bad tip, that's all."

"So, that's why you couldn't even make a first payment?"

"Y…y…yes, Mr. Jimmy. I swear it. But I'll make it up. I promise. I…I'll pay it all back…right away."

"We don't need you to pay the whole thing back right away. We want what's left of the money. We'll talk about the rest, later."

"No…no…you don't understand. It's all gone. All of it."

The Geek put the muzzle between Joe's eyes. "This is it, asshole. If you ain't got any of it, then there's no reason for you to live, now is there?"

"I…I did nothing to deserve this," Joe cried, and shaking like a Chevy Corvair running on five cylinders. "I already paid you guys back by shooting Sally Boy! You know I did, you know? What's a guy gotta do to prove himself around here, huh? I have a sick mother, you know? I never wanted to leave. I had to. I'm loyal to the gang, I tell ya. I had no one else to take care of her, you know? What's more, I had amnesia. I can get the money…all of it. Give me a little more time. A little time is all I need. I'll show you, you know? Just give me a little…"

"Yeah, I know, toilet breath," the Geek barked. Here…take this you stupid fuck!"

"Okay, okay…I'll tell ya where…"

(FUMPH…FUMPH…FUMPH)

"And here's another one for your mother! You know?"

(FUMPH)

"Damn, you pretty near blew his head clean off," said Tommy, his mouth wide open as he leaned over to gape at the broken pieces left of Barnes' scull.

"Yup! like a snake caught in a lawn mower," said Fast Eddie. "Hey, youz guys know what I'm tinkin'? Didn't it sound like the ol' Barnes wuz about ta tell us where da money was?"

"Nah! You think so?" said The Geek.

"I don't know. He wuz gabbin' so much, I nearly dozed off, but I think he wuz startin' to say somethin' jus' when ya pulled the trigga."

"I think I heard it, too," said Tommy.

"Too late now," said The Geek. "And don't mention that part to the boss, or we'll all wind up floating down the river."

"Ya want for us to dump'm in dis here lake, Big Jimmy?" Tommy asked.

Eddie butted in. "Waddya stupid? What da fuck for? Dems cops is gonna find'm anyways."

The Geek left them to find a place to bury the gun.

"We could tie some cinda blocks to his feet. I saw that in the movies once." Tommy said to Eddie.

"Ayyy, fugedit! Like we's gots time to go to a hardware staw and pick up a coupla cinda blocks. He's only gonna float to da top when he fills up wid gas."

"Where's he gonna get gas from," Tommy asked?"

Eddie smirked while flashing a quick glance at the night sky. "At da gas station, bwittle bwain. Jeesh! We gotta lose dis guy!"

"Shaddup, Eddie! An' what da hell is a bwittle bwain, anyway?"

Pointing to his head, Eddie shot back, "Dats what yooze gots upsteahs... lotsa peanut bwittle."

"Oh gee, Eddie. Is there a remote possibility that maybe ya might be tryin' to say…brittle brain?"

"Youz knows exactly what I means, Mista English teacha, da nut job."

"Fuck you, Eddie."

"Fuck you, too, and your colored momma."

"Fuck your momma, too, Eddie."

"Well den fuck your momma what's puts out for all o' da colored boys and takes it up da…"

Jimmy returned and stepped between them. "Hey, hey! Stop arguing, you two knuckle-heads!"

Tommy stuck his head out from behind the side of Jimmy's huge body and pointed back at Eddie with a beginning of tears. "Your momma, too, Eddie, and don't be talkin' about my mamma like dat."

"Aw golly molly, did I hoit your feelin's, Tommy wit da momma dats got no teets in 'er head and da long line o' colored boys linin' up around da block for a gum job."

"I said shut up and stop arguing, before I plug the both of you. Two more isn't going to matter, you hear me?"

"Okay, Jimmy boy," said Eddie. "Ain't no problem." He pointed back at Tommy. "Your momma still sucks colored boys, ol' bwittle bwain Tommy, da wise ass wit peanut bwittle fa bwains and who ain't got no..."

"What did I just say, you stupid idiot." The Geek gave Eddie a shove that nearly sent him all the way to Astoria Blvd. "Now shut up the both of you. Did any of you think to look through his pockets?"

"That's a good idea, I'll check," said Tommy, wiping the tears with his sleeve. "Here's his wallet, a pack of Lucky Strikes and, ah…only two cigarettes left though. Some change. Oh, a gold ring on his finga, looks like."

"Give it here," said Jimmy."

"It won't come off!"

"Den cut his finga off, stupid," said Fast Eddie.

Tommy took out a switch blade and sawed off Joe's finger.

Grabbing the ring and wallet, The Geek said, "This'll keep them from finding out who he is for a while longer. What else is in his pockets?"

"I'm lookin'! I'm lookin'! A set o' keys. Here ya go, Big Jimmy."

The Geek caught them. "Fantastic! Now get in the car, we're all going for a ride."

"Where to, Big Jimmy?"

"Brooklyn!"

8:03 P.M.
240 Dean Street
Diego's Apartment

"Did you have a nice time with Mr. Richards?"

"We had a great time, Mom," Said Diego. "I like the brontosaurus. You wouldn't believe how big that thing was. What's wrong, Mom? You don't look so good."

"It's my hip. I'm in a lot of pain today."

"I find it hard to believe that you went dancing with Popi years ago."

"Every Saturday at Roseland in the city, and him with a wooden leg."

"I'll put the radio on for you."

"Put on that nice station I always like to hear, 97, I think it is."

"All right, Mom. I'm sure glad you're not asking for that Le Lo Li, Island music, again."

The radio warmed up, screeching back as Diego turned the dial until clearing into *Dancing Cheek to Cheek* being sung by Louie Armstrong and Ella Fitzgerald.

(Heaven…I'm in heaven…and the cares that hung around me…)

"You don't like Puerto Rican music?" Ana asked. "It's good latin music."

"Not really and I'm not crazy about this one either. It's old stuff from the fifties. I hate when they stick them in like this, especially after a good song. You want me to change it?"

"No, I like this song. Its one of the songs me and your Poppa use to dance to."

The song brought Ana back to a time of deep nurtured love when life was at its fullest. Back then, long black, wavy hair flowed to her waist like a fabled princess. It was a time of light heeled dance with a soul mate she shared everything with. Now, all she had left of his legacy was their shared child, a gift she still worshipped him for. She missed him terribly. And how could their son ever know what she still felt inside for him—the missing, the tears, the loneliness, the forever lost love she now had to endure without?

"Mom, as long as you like it, I'll leave it on."

"Si, I like it. Now come dance with your mamita, Diego."

"Aw, that's so silly."

"No its not! Come dance with me."

"What about your hip?"

"It's okay. I'm not worried about the pain. Come dance before the song finishes."

With one hand gripping the edge of the table and the other holding onto the back of a chair, Ana inched herself along until she stood half bent over in the aisle.

(…climb a mountain and reach the highest peak, but it wouldn't thrill me half as much as dancing cheek to cheek.)

She let go of the chair, took a short step forward and reached out for her son. "Come! Spin me around and let's see what we can do."

"Yeah, sure, Mom. Just be careful."

(Oh, when we're out together...)

Ana stumbled, tried to catch herself and fell into Diego's outstretched arms.

(As when we're dancing cheek to cheek.)

"See that! How do you expect to dance? Why don't you sit down on the couch and I'll stay and listen to the radio with you?"

"Oh, Diego!" Ana play slapped him on the arm. "Now dance and listen to the song."

(...highest peak, but It wouldn't be half as much...)

He held his mother by the waist and turned her in a slow circle.

"No, Diego! You have to touch my cheek...like the song says to do." She grabbed the back of his head and pushed his cheek into hers. "See, I told you we could do it?"

"Yeah...right!"

"Now, listen to the pretty words. When me and you are outside together, we can dance together, you and I."

"I don't think those are the exact words, Mom."

"If it didn't bother your poppa, then it should not bother you. Dame un besito, mi muneco."

"Diego kissed his mother on the cheek like she asked, then helped her to the couch. "Mom, why are you so afraid of doctors?"

"Because they did nothing for your poppa."

"Well, that wasn't the doctor's fault, was it?"

"I think it was. They don't know anything."

"That's not very scientific."

"I done care if it's not scientific and I'm too tired now to talk about it."

"You really need to go to a clinic. At least let them take a look. I'll go with you...please?"

"No, I'm too afraid."

8:32 P.M.
Outside Diego's building

"Leave the car double parked," said Jimmy the Geek. "This won't take long."

The three entered the building and rushed up the stairs to the top floor. At 2B, The Geek turned the key and pushed the door open.

"I'll search under the mattress."

Eddie pointed at the bureau. "Hey Tommy, go check da drawers."

"Oh, yeah? And what're you gonna do, Eddie?"

"I'm gonna stay ova hear and play wit my winky. Whaddya tink I'm gonna do, boid bwain? Doesn't ya sees me headin' for da closet wid dem cross eyed peepers of yaws?"

"Yeah, I can see where ya headin'. And what winky are ya talkin' 'bout? Not dat short, teenie weenie worm whats in your pants, I hope."

"Well, at least it ain't as short as yours. Is that why ya pees on your balls everytime ya goes to da baretroom?"

"How would you know? Was ya salivaten while you was watchin'?"

The Geek's voice resonated loud and clear. "Are you two going to start that arguing again? Let's go! Find the money!"

"Nope, nuttin' in the bureau," said Tommy, leaving all five drawers opened.

"Then check under the carpet!"

"Now how do I do that, Big Jimmy, wit' youz two guys standin' on it and alla dis furnicha what's here?"

"No, not the whole thing. Pull up the corners," the Geek replied, shaking his head.

Fast Eddie, quipped, "Yeah, woach bwain, maybe you'll find some of youz's long lost relatives under dere."

Jimmy shouted at the both of them. "Shut the hell up, you two knuckle-heads and keep lookin'."

"Yeah, yeah!" Eddie buried his head inside the closet. Soon, his muffled voice returned from behind the clothes rack. "Hey, ya know what I foun'?"

Hopeful, The Geek looked up.

"Dere's a pencil size whole in da wall what's looks right ova da topada tub. Hey, dis guy was a freakin,' peepin' Tommy."

"Hey, watch that!" said Tommy.

"Yeah, wudda sleeze bag. Hey, whaddya say we wait and see if some chick uses da turly bowl? Huh? Whaddy say, fellas?"

"Check the clothes and stay focused," said Jimmy. "There's gotta be something in here." He turned to the TV and ripped the back panel off to search inside. He did the same for the radio. "Tommy! Ain't you finished yet? Check his shoes and those boxes over there." Jimmy stood in front of the window and checked behind the curtain. "When you two get done, get out into the hall and look around. I'll be in the bathroom."

As soon as Jimmy entered the hall, the door to 2A slowly closed shut.

"What the hell were **you** lookin' at?" He barked.

He approached the door and knocked. No answer. He knocked again, a little louder this time. Still no answer. By now, the other two joined him in the hall to see what all the noise was about.

"Somebody awfully nosy lives behind this door."

"Are ya gonna kick it in, Big Jimmy?" asked Tommy.

"Hey, are you two finished in there?"

"Ain't nuttin' left in dat room, not even a rat's butt," said Eddie.

"Then look in the rest of the hallway like I told you."

Jimmy banged on the door again. "Hey you in there! You didn't hear nothing! Got it?"

Entering the bathroom, the first place he searched was under the lid to the toilet tank. Finding it empty, he unraveled a strip of toilet paper from the roll and loosely balled it up. Striking a match, he lit the paper and tossed it under the claw foot tub. Other than dust balls, a toothpaste cap, used Q-tips yellow with ear wax and cigarette butts, there was nothing else. He lit another and threw it underneath, just to make sure.

Next, he pulled the mirror off the wall and turned the waste basket upside down.

"There's nothing in this room, either."

"Whaddya wanna do, Big Jimmy?" said Tommy.

"Come on! I guess we gotta go tell Spillane."

The Geek got as far as the stairway where he tightened his grip on the banister. He scratched day old whiskers while giving the whole thing more thought. "I can't believe he spent all of that money. What time is it?"

Fast Eddie checked. "8:44!"

The huge man shook his head. "The money's gotta be up here somewhere. You know what? There's one more place we haven't checked."

"2A?" said Fast Eddie.

"Yeah...2A!"

The Geek leaned over the railing and looked down.

"Whaddya gonna do?" said Tommy.

"Watch!" Lifting his foot, the Geek gave the door one solid shot that sent it slamming into the room and a row of full boxes stacked against the inside wall.

"**EEEEEEEEE!**" Mary screamed. She toppled over backwards from the impact of the door to her face and then hit the floor with a loud thud.

"Dumb broad!" said The Geek. "That's what you get for lookin' through the keyhole. Hey Eddie, put a gag on her mouth. And you…keep your mouth shut lady, or you ain't gonna have a head on your shoulders to yell from anymore."

"I…I have eight dollars and some change in my purse. Take it and anything else…mm, mm, mph…"

"Tighter! Make it tighter! Now give her some room. Let her sit in that chair." Jimmy's arms folded as he gave her a long look of disgust.

Gasping on the floor for breath, Mary, wearing an over washed, cotton house dress with nothing underneath, slowly turned around on her knees with her hairy butt facing the opened doorway."

"Nice…real nice," said Fast Eddie, his head lowered and turned to the side for a better look.

Gradually, Mary struggled to her feet, staggered to an overstuffed recliner and dropped heavily into it, the impact, slamming the recliner into the wall behind.

The Geek pulled up a wooden chair from the table and sat directly in front of her collapsed body, crammed into the cushions like an oversized clam too big for its shell. He lit a cigar, shook the match and threw it onto the floor. Taking a long, slow drag, he exhaled with no thought as to direction, and with a sympathetic sounding voice, said, "Look lady, I'm only gonna say this once. We want the money and we think it's in here. Now, you can be a nice fat lady and tell us where it is, or I'm gonna get awfully mad. Now, what's it gonna be?"

Mary stared back, her reddened eyes glistening like glazed cherries. She cowered as far into the recliner as she could possibly get while meekly looking back at the large man in front of her."

"Okay lady…I'm gonna take this gag off and no screaming…ya got that?" She nodded.

"Now…what's your name?"

"M-M-Mary…Mary."

"Mary, Mary, or just Mary?"

"Just M-Mary. Wh…what do you boys want? All I have is…"

"Yeah, yeah, we heard the one about the eight bucks, already. We want the big money. The $10,000 Barnes gave you to hold for him."

"Who…who's Barnes?"

"Oh, come on lady. The guy that lives in 2B. Your boyfriend, maybe?"

"2B? No….that, that's not my boyfriend. I..I didn't even know that was his last name. I only know him as Joe. All we ever said to one another was… maybe hello and that was only when I used the bathroo…"

"Man, this broad is so full o' shit." The Geek stood up and held onto the back of the chair. "You know what boys? I think we gotta waste the fat lady."

"Please. I'm telling you the truth. Look around all you want," she cried.

The Geek sucked in a drag and took a quick look around at all the clutter. The room had enough to fill a garbage truck. Any available floor space besides the main walkways, between the front door, the bed, and the window, was taken up by boxes and stacks of books or folded up clothes.

He twisted the cigar into the armrest, snuffing it out. Grabbing both arms firmly, he leaned forward. His huge head hovered above hers for a brief moment and then slowly lowered until his nose was barely an inch away from hers. It made her visibly shake uncontrollably. Tears streamed down her cheeks, the mucous, trickling onto her upper lip.

Broken, she blurted out, "I…I really don't know anything. Besides, how much money do you think I really need to live in this place? I don't go anywhere. I stay in this room all the time. I don't even go downstairs."

Fast Eddie said, "Oh yeah, den how do ya get your gwossries lady…by air mail? Jeesh!"

"Well, no…the kids…I…I give them a nickel and they…" Stopping in mid-sentence, she turned away from Fast Eddie to face the Geek; whose big head was once again barely an inch away from hers. Gasping, she jerked backwards into the cushions.

"Man, dis lady's a cry baby just like the Barnes wuz," said Fast Eddie.

"Was?" Mary asked, red faced and inadvertently blowing bubbles from her nostrils while shrinking from the Geek?

"Yeah…was, like you're gonna be," the Geek said. "Now, come clean and tell us what you know?"

"Please…check the whole room if you want. I…I never had anything to do with him. That's the God's honest truth."

"What about the other room, lady…room 2C?"

"Nobody's been in that room for months."

"Go check it out Tommy, while me and Fast Eddie here have a pleasant little chat with Joe's girlfriend."

"Please, I wasn't his girlfriend. It wasn't that way at all."

"Yeah, sure!" The Geek approached the window and looked down below at the 12 stone steps of the front stoop. "I had enough of this horse shit. Let's dump Mary Mary out this window, Fast Eddie."

"Ohhh, my God! Oh, please, please!"

Eddie showed a worried look on his face. "Ya know what, Big Jimmy? I really don't think she knows any-ting, I really don't." He nervously unwrapped a Bazooka, tossed the gum into his mouth and furiously began chewing. "Nah, she don't know nuttin'."

The Geek's head jerked around. "Yo! Meathead! Shut up, already! Whose doing the interrogating around here, you or me?" He took another look through the window, grinned and said, "Hey, that'd be something to see, huh? Imagine that…this big blimp hitting the stoop all the way down there like a big, fat, juicy watermelon?"

His eyes shifted back and forth as he took quick glances at Mary.

"Ah…yeah, it wouldn't be no problem for me, neither. We don't even have to open it…just ram ol' fatty, Mary Mary's ass right through this glass."

"Ohhh!" Mary lowered her face into her lap, sobbing and shaking with her hands covering her head.

"This is your last chance lady. Where's the money? Tell us where it is and we'll leave you alone."

"Please! I don't know where the money is." (*Sob! Sniffle! Snort!*)

"Hey…forget it! Come on Eddie, let's check the rest of the room out."

The Geek grabbed a towel and tossed it to Mary. "Wipe that snot off your face. I'm tired of lookin' at it."

Starting at the far corner, Big Jimmy threw books onto the floor and spilled boxes open. The closet was particularly hard to get to. Eddie had to up-end furniture and dump them on top of one another. Once inside, he threw everything from the closet back into the room, checking pockets and shoes or anything with enough room inside to conceal money.

"That other room is empty," said Tommy, a cigarette hanging from his lips upon stepping through the open doorway. "Yup, I checked under the carpet, too, like you told me to do in Barnes' room, right Big Jimmy? Ya want me to cut her?"

The Geek frowned. "Why is it that I'm getting awfully tired of you?"

"Who me, Big Jimmy?"

"Yeah, you! Okay, listen up. I don't think the broad knows anything. I mean...look at her. Does that look like something the Barnes would go for?"

"No, not really," said Fast Eddie, eying Mary scrunched into the recliner.

The Geek rubbed his jaw. "Look...we already checked behind door number one and the bathroom, right?"

"Right!"

"Right!"

We also checked behind door number two, this door, and there's nothing behind here either. So it's gotta be behind another door?"

"Door number three!" Eddie pointedly answered. Da empty room what's across da hall?" (*Snap...Chew...Chew*)

"No, not that door! Tommy already checked that one. The Door Barnes took with him to the grave."

"Oh, yeah, dat door!" said Tommy.

"Door numba four! Da race track!" said Fast Eddie. (*Snap...Pop*)

"Exactly, said Jimmy. "That's what I was thinking. Come on...let's get the hell out of here. We wasted enough time."

Mary felt overwhelmed with relief. They were finally leaving.

"Remember! We were never here," the Geek said, pointing his finger at her. "And don't forget what I told you about the window, so keep your trap shut."

"I won't say anything," she said, blowing her nose and wiping her eyes.

Eddie lingered behind. Hearing Tommy go down the steps behind the Geek, he turned to Mary and as nicely as he could put it, or with as much finesse as a frog, said, "Ya knows what Mary? I knew yas didn't know nuttin' 'bout no money." (*Snap*) "See...dat's why I kinda laid back like and didn't say nuttin' bad. I was protectin' ya, I really was, see?" (*Snap...Pop*) "So whaddy say I come back a liddle layda for a liddle...ah, you know, a liddle tumble? Well? Waddya say?"

"Oh, please leave me alone. Please!" Mary murmured beneath her sobs.

"Aw, come on chubsy wubsy, don't be like dat. Look...I like big fat tubs like you, Mary. Youz is my kinda gal. So howza 'boudit, you and me, you know…jus' a little roll 'n' da hay, huh? Whaddya say? Is it woit a nice yummy piece o' chawclit cake to ya? Huh?" (*Snicker…Snap…Pop Chew…Chew*)

"Oh, go already! Leave me alone!"

"Oh, yeah?" Eddie spit the gum out. "Well I got a lotta dames back in the city, see? I can get anybody I wants. I don't need da likes of you, no-hows, ya crazy bwoad."

He stomped loudly to the open doorway where he suddenly stopped and ran his fingers through his hair. Pausing for a long moment, he lowered his head and then turned around with a defeated and somewhat remorseful look at Mary's limp body. His gaze dropped to the floor as he slowly reached around for his wallet.

"Here! Takes dis ten spot for all da trouble."

He let the bill drop to the floor and left for the stairs without closing the door. On the way down, his singing amplified throughout the hallway.

"My Bonnie lies ova da mountin'. My Bonnie lies ova da sea. My Bonnie lies ova da mountin'. So bring back my Bonnie to me, to me. So, bring back by Bonnie to me."

Sunday

Detective Ted Williams opened the front gate to 240 Dean Street. He acknowledged the patrolmen standing by at the bottom of the stoop and made his way to the top floor.

"What time ya got?" He asked Detective Don O'Brien, who had been waiting for him outside the locked door to 2B.

"Two o'clock!"

"Two? My watch stopped. Whaddya got so far?"

O'Brien aimed his thumb at the door behind him. "The fingerprint guys are still in there dusting. So far they found four sets. Let's go into the back room, there's a lady right there in 2A."

Det. O'Brien let Williams walk ahead of him into 2C, the vacant room at the back of the hall before closing the door.

"Are you saying there were four besides the guy that lives here?" Ted asked.

"No, that includes him."

"Boy…headquarters sure found out who this Barnes guy was pretty fast."

"Yeah, well, they found a pay stub in his shirt pocket. He's got a rap sheet a mile long. The body was already stiff when they found it. The boat people discovered the body a little before ten when they opened up this morning."

"So, that puts the time of death somewhere around…what…early last night? Say, do you think it has something to do with that hit in Little Italy?"

"Sally Boy Rinaldi? It's got everything to do with that. Doesn't headquarters ever tell you anything?" Detective O'Brien quipped.

"I came from the house. I was on swing shift all week. Captain called me on the phone to brief me on the case. I came straight here."

"Well…anyway, right now we got more witnesses then the Jehovah's. Red 59 Chevy with Jersey plates. Four guys inside with Tommy McBride at the wheel."

Williams noted the broken mirror and spilled garbage on the bathroom floor. "Who I-D'd the driver?"

"Somebody in the restaurant. One of Sally boy's buddies. He also described a huge guy jumping into the car after the shots rang out, followed by Barnes, the shooter."

"Tommy McBride! Ain't that one of Spillane's boys?"

"That's right. "But lots of luck getting him in for an interview."

"Why's that, don't he like Brooklyn?" As Ted said that, he checked underneath the tub.

"Apparently he must have loved Brooklyn! They found him floating belly up on this side of the bridge a few hours ago. He was dead for a while, sometime late last night or very early this morning."

Reaching under the tub, Ted fingered the black residue from burned toilet paper. "Same as that Barnes guy!" He smelled his fingers.

"Right! And guess what?"

"What?"

"He's not gonna look too good to his relatives when they visit his coffin."

"Oh?"

Don grimaced. "Eels ate what was left of his brains where he was shot. His whole head was caved in. Recycled part of his last meal of pizza, too."

Williams shook his head. "Wow…that's going to be a closed casket for sure. Damn! A triple hit. Humph! They wanted to keep Tommy quiet! Apparently, Spillane figured that out ahead of time. That's why they put him in the driver's seat. People were bound to see who was driving, and Tommy of course was expendable. I guess he wasn't worth much to them."

"Nope! A little too low on the totem pole…like the two of us, huh, Ted?"

"Very funny…speak for yourself. I'm happy where I am. Hey Don, you know what else?"

"No, what?"

"This ain't gonna go down easy. The 18th Precinct over in Manhattan isn't going to give up Spillane or any of his crony gang members."

Don Agreed. "Not if their captain wants to get home to Forest Hills in one piece."

"Right, and I'm pretty sure that's a nice monthly check he gets from Spillane, enough to pay my mortgage and then some. By the way…did you interview anybody in the building, yet?"

"Yeah, the lady in the front room. She says she never heard anything."

"She never heard anything?" Ted cracked the door, looked out and quickly shut it. "Then how the hell did the frame of her door get broken like that without her knowing? Or this one!" As he said that, he pulled off a piece of split molding from the door jamb.

O'Brien shrugged and spread his hands in the air. "I'm only telling' you what she told me."

"I suppose she didn't hear that bathroom mirror getting ripped off the wall, either?"

"I know, but she's not talking."

"Didn't you threaten to take her to the station?"

"She's a big lady, Ted. I wouldn't know how to get her there. Maybe you better go on in and question her for yourself? You might have better luck."

"What about the rest of the house?"

"As you can see, this room's empty. I haven't been downstairs, but it's clear from the looks of things on this floor that these guys were searching for something."

"Yeah! So, how do you want to write this up…as a burglary?"

"No, not yet! So far, I'm waiting for forensics. All I have is a few notes. I was also waiting for you so we could interview everybody else in the building. I figured we'd go together. You know, for a little added pressure."

"So, you wanna go back in there?" said Ted.

"The front room? Nah! I wasn't talking about the lady in 2A. I meant the people downstairs. This one here is about to have a nervous breakdown. You go...you might have better luck."

"Okay Don, then go on ahead and I'll meet you on the first floor when I'm done."

"Right."

"Oh, and Don?"

"Yeah?"

"Maybe we better hold off on the report for a while. Both precincts might want to white wash this whole thing before the mayor makes a thing of it and sticks his nose in."

"You're right. It ain't like any of these guys are gonna be missed. Not by the good citizens of New York, at least."

"Exactly! And you know what else?"

"What's that?"

"We got to find out whatever it was that was so important, three guys had to die for it. I'd hate to see any more of this spill across the river."

Before Don O'Brien got halfway down the stairs, the door to Barnes' room opened.

"Hi, Ted. We're all done in there...and in the bathroom as well, in case you want to check that out."

"I already did, Carl. What did you find in Barnes' room?"

"Besides his prints, we got three sets and all of them in places thieves would be."

"So it was a burglary?"

"I don't think so. At least not in the usual sense of the word. Whoever it was, they had a key. It was still in the lock when we got here. They ripped open the back of the TV and the radio, so, it's a cinch they weren't lookin' to pawn anything. All of the drawers in the bureau were pulled out and the mattress was out of place."

"Sounds like a burglary to me."

"Okay, I guess you should know. You're the detective, not me."

"Unless they got the dead guy's permission to ransack his room," Ted joked. "So, then, you believe, that they were definitely looking for something specific."

"Right...that's what we figured."

"Okay Carl. I'll meet you back at headquarters."

"Don't look for any results today. Check with us tomorrow, we might have something for you by noon."

"Sure, otherwise call me right away. You have my house number?"

"Yeah, I got it, I'll call you."

(KNOCK...KNOCK...KNOCK)

"Yes?" Mary's soft voice responded from behind the door.

"Detective Williams, Ma'am."

"I already spoke to someone."

"I know lady, but I need to tie up a few things."

"I don't want to talk to anyone."

"Lady, a guy in your building has been murdered. Either you talk to me now or I get a court order and come back in an hour. Which will it be?"

Ted waited for an answer for a long, intermittent silence. "Well?" He finally said.

"The doors broken. Go ahead and push it. It's unlocked."

The detective stepped inside to the disarray of the room.

"Have a seat by the table. I'm sorry about the mess in here," she said.

Ted could see exactly what Don had meant. She sure was a big woman. "That's quite a shiner you got there."

Mary self conscientiously covered her right eye. "I fell."

"Look lady! Oh, I'm sorry, I didn't get your name?"

"Mary."

"Mary, I'm Detective Williams. Feel free to call me Ted."

"Why are all the cops still here?"

"Didn't the other detective tell you?"

"About Joe?

"Right...Joe!"

"Yes, I know. He was the guy they found in Central Park. They were talking all morning on the radio about finding a body there. I was surprised when they finally mentioned where he lived."

"That's right, Mary, and I think there's a little bit more you do know."

"Like what?"

"All right, Mary...let's stop beating around the bush with this thing. Something happened in your room last night. How did your door get broken?"

"I…I, um…it was already that way. It's been broken a long time. Like the one downstairs. The landlord never fixes anything around here. He just collects the rent and complains about us. It **was** that way. I swear it wa…"

"Oh, really? So, what about the bathroom? I suppose you didn't hear a noise in there, either?"

"No, I didn't!"

"That's it, lady! I had just about enough of this. You're coming downtown with me for aiding and abetting."

Mary smiled facetiously as she leaned back into the recliner, her elbows resting on the armrests. She tapped her fingertips together in front of her face and with a relaxed demeanor, said, "And how do you propose to do that, Mr. Williams?"

"With a crane if I have to. We'll remove this window and hoist you down to the street and drop you into a damn dump truck, if need be. And don't believe we won't do that"

Mary covered her mouth. "Oh, my God! That's what he said."

"What?"

"That Geek guy said he was going to shove me out of the window."

"If you're involved in any way shape or form, I'll have you arrested."

"Involved with who?"

"Did you have some kind of a relationship with Barnes or the guys who broke your door in?"

"No!"

"Okay…then, were these guys mad at you for something, like something you did or said?"

"They asked me if Joe was my boyfriend and I told them no. Oh, my God! I'm going to get killed."

"Nobody's going to do anything to you, Mary. That's why we're here. To protect you."

"I'm dead. That's it. My life is over. These guys are going to come back and finish the job."

"Now you're getting ridiculous. Unless there's something you're not telling me. Which is everything at the moment."

"I can't help it, I'm frightened. They told me not to say anything."

"I understand, Mary. That's why we need to find out who was in this room and we think one of them is already dead."

"Joe?"

"No, I'm not talking about Joe…well, him, too, but I meant one of the other guys. One of the men that was in your room last night."

"Oh…I see?"

"Hey, look…we're here to protect you. I don't want you to have to worry about anyone coming back to hurt you."

"Detective Williams, these guys were awfully scary. I can't even lock my door anymore and the one downstairs stays open all the time. I slept on the floor next to the door last night so it wouldn't get pushed in. I didn't sleep a wink."

"You said…these guys. How many were there?"

"Um…I only saw three."

"Could there have been more than that?"

"I don't know, that's all I saw."

"How did you see them the first time? Did you open the door to look out?"

"I looked through the keyhole."

"As far as that broken door is concerned? I have to go downstairs in a little while to talk to the landlord. I'll get him to fix both doors."

"He never fixes anything around here."

"He will when I tell him. Otherwise, I'll have the beat cop write him up for litter or for as many violations as he can think of, and we can do that every day of the week. He'll comply!"

"That's kind of you, Detective."

"So, what time was it when you first heard a noise?"

"Ah…it was about a half hour before the Ed Sullivan Show came on. So, probably around 8:30."

Williams' lips scrunched tightly together. "So, you looked through the keyhole and what did you see?"

Embarrassed, Mary stared at the floor. "They were in Joe's room talking."

"What about?"

"Mostly about where to look. I smelled paper burning when the big guy was in the bathroom."

"The burnt tissue under the bathtub. He did that so he could see underneath it. Go on. What happened after that?"

"The guy they called Big Jimmy, or the Geek, knocked on my door and threatened me."

"So, what time would you say that was?"

"Around ten to nine."

"What did he say?"

"He said to keep my mouth shut, or something like that."

"Good. You're doing real good, Mary?"

"You will talk to the landlord, won't you, Detective Williams?"

"As soon as I get downstairs. O'Brien is down there right now waiting for me. He's the detective that spoke to you earlier."

"Yes, I know. Can I offer you a soda?"

"No thank you."

Ted got up and crossed to where Mary sat leaning into the easy chair. Squatting in front, he looked at her with a kind and long lashed, green eyed gaze while taking her hand in his.

"I really need you to tell me everything, Mary."

Ted's voice sounded soft and smooth. "It's important and I don't care how small you might think it is. If you remember anything, you need to tell me, right now. Otherwise, I won't be able to help you, okay? Now, let's start with the door. How did it get broken?"

Mary sighed. "They...well...um..."

"Take your time, Mary."

"They came back."

"Who came back?"

"The guy that knocked on the door."

"The Big Jimmy guy you mentioned and the ones with him?"

"Yes, that's right."

"How soon?"

"A few minutes later."

"Go on."

"Well...they kicked my door in, the Big Jimmy guy, I mean. He was the one who kicked the door in."

Ted took a quick look at the door. "So you were behind the keyhole and that's how you got your black eye?"

Mary stared out the window. "Yeah, I guess so."

"You're lucky, Mary."

"Lucky?" She turned back to him.

"They could have killed you."

"Yes, I know, but why?"

"Obviously, you were a witness since you saw their faces and heard their names, right?"

"You're really scaring me."

"I'm sorry, Mary. Actually, they have nothing to gain by coming back to this place. Not anymore. In fact, I have a feeling that this Jimmy guy is long gone and out of town by now, like Chicago or Boston. And guess what?"

"What?"

"We're the biggest gang in New York."

"Who?"

"Us! The police…and we're on your side. That's why I need to know everything you know."

"I'll try."

"What happened next?"

"Well…they thought I was Joe's girlfriend and that I was holding money for him. That's what they wanted. That's what they were looking for. Ten thousand dollars."

"Ten thousand? Okay…please, go on."

"He said…"

"Who said?"

"The Big Jimmy, guy. He said he was going to throw me out of the window like a big, fat watermelon." Mary wiped the sudden flush of tears from her eyes and thought for a minute before continuing. "Or a juicy watermelon, or something like that. God, I was so frightened. He was so scary. He left his cigar behind. I threw it in the trash."

"Did you hear any of the other names mentioned, besides him?"

"Yes! Tommy and a skinny guy named Fast Eddie."

"Did you say Tommy?" Ted rubbed the corners of his mouth with a thought. *Tommy McBride! That clinches it.*

"If I showed you a picture of this Tommy character, would you be able to identify him?"

"Of course! He was right here in this room."

"Okay…so a bunch of guys, three you said, but you weren't exactly sure, came upstairs the first time around eight thirty or so. They looked around the other rooms, you smelled smoke and then they knocked on your door around ten to nine, right?"

"Yes!"

"And that's when they threatened for you not to say anything?"

"Mm, hm!"

"A few minutes after that they kicked the door in, at which point you saw only three men."

"Yes."

"So, to the best of your knowledge, what time did they leave?"

"I think 9:20 or 9:30. I was pretty upset."

"Yes, I'm sure you were."

"As you can see, they turned the place upside down. This will take months to straighten out."

"Obviously, they must have believed you. About the money, that is. There's a code within the mob circle not to hurt women and children. Unless, of course it's absolutely necessary. That and the fact that they finally realized you had nothing to do with Barnes or the money must have satisfied them.

"All right Mary, I'm going downstairs. I don't want to bother you anymore with this. At least for now. Here's my number. What's yours, in case I have to call you?"

"Ulster 5-3189."

If you think of anything, would you call me?"

"Yes, I sure will, Detective. Thanks for the help with the doors."

"Don't mention it, and don't worry about them coming back. There's nothing for them to come back to, okay?"

"Okay."

"Hey, besides, with all the names we have, and the recent murders, the rest of Barnes's associates are going to remain low for quite a while."

"Murders? Three?"

"Put the news on. I'm sure they caught up by now. We have a cop downstairs by the front stoop. I'll make sure he stays until the doors get fixed."

"Uh…Detective Williams?"

"Yes?"

"I feel so much better…thank you."

"Before I go, you said the cigar was in the waste basket?"

"Yes, by the door."

The detective took a handkerchief out of his jacket pocket, reached in and moved a few papers out of the way. Eying the cigar, he grabbed it carefully and rolled it up inside the cloth."

Downstairs, The door to 1B was open when he got there. "How's everything going?"

"We just finished winding everything up," said O'Brien. "You ready to interview 1A?"

"I'm right behind you."

(KNOCK…KNOCK)

"By the way," said Williams, "the lady upstairs mentioned a Tommy as being one of the guys that broke into her apartment."

"The floater under the bridge!"

"Probably! At any rate, we'll know tomorrow when the prints come back. She also mentioned Fast Eddie."

"Another one of Spillane's boys."

"Right…and you ever hear of a guy named The Geek, Jimmy the Geek, or Big Jimmy?"

"That's news to me. No, not really."

A Pause, and then Ted asked, "What did you find out in there?"

"Nah, nothing! She was too scared to open the door last night."

Ted nodded. "Like the one upstairs. Then, she must have heard the noise?"

"Oh, for sure, before nine. I wrote down 8:45. She remembers because she was afraid the kids would wake up with all the banging, knowing they had to go to school this morning. She heard a bunch of heavy footsteps when the men left around a half hour later.

(More knocking)

"It doesn't look like any…"

The door to 1A opened.

"Hello? I'm sorry, but I have a problem with my hip. You are the police?"

"Yes, ma'am. May we come in?" Said Detective Williams.

"Surely. Please…sit down. Can I pour you some coffee?"

"No thank you. This is Detective O'Brien and I'm Detective Williams. We're here to gather a little info about the guy upstairs."

As Ted said that, Don flipped a notebook to a blank page.

"Yes…Joe. I know him," Ana replied.

"How well did you know him?"

"Not very well. I stayed inside most of the day. I don't go outside very often. Like I said before, I have a bad hip. That's why I took as long as I did to answer the door."

"I understand."

"I saw Joe yesterday, detective."

"Oh…when? I mean what time?"

"It was about 1:30 in the afternoon."

"What made you remember?"

"My son, Diego. He left to go to the museum with Mister Richards. He had to meet him before twelve. It was after that. I don't remember exactly. I'm thinking maybe around 1:20 or 1:30."

"Who is Mr. Richards?"

"The assemblyman. I went outside to ask the girls to go to the store for me. Joe was sitting on the stoop drinking coffee. Excuse me. May I go to the bathroom? Would that be okay?"

"Sure, not a problem." Ted waited for the door to close. "Hey, do you think she had something going on with Barnes?"

"That's kind of a stretch, don't you think?"

"Why, she's a pretty lady. In this business nothing's a stretch. You'll learn that after you get as much time in as I have. I'm not surprised by anything anymore."

Don nibbled his lower lip in thought. "She says she saw him around 1:20 in the afternoon."

"So!"

"Okay….so we know Barnes showed up at work around two from his time card. Besides that, the last person to see him at the theatre was the lady behind the concession counter. I checked that out earlier."

Ted nodded with half interest. "And?"

"No….nothing. I'm looking for a time line, that's all. We know he was on Grand Street a little after seven, when Sally Boy got hit, right?"

Williams smirked. "And Barnes got hit sometime late the same day. So what?"

"Not much, I guess, except, why would he even show up at work if he knew he was going to be making a hit in the city at seven?"

"That's easy. He needed an alibi."

"But no one saw him in the theatre after 2:30. That leaves four and half hours unaccounted for. That's quite a lot of time. Even if he took a subway, it takes, what, maybe a half hour to get to the Village from downtown Brooklyn, and we know he was in a car...the red Chevy."

Detective Williams shrugged that off. "If the witnesses are correct, then yes, you're right, which means he screwed up his alibi. That only makes him stupid. So maybe they went bowling. Who cares? Does it really matter what he was doing in between? Unless there was another hit somewhere else, it doesn't concern me. Anyway, there wasn't. The rest of the city was quiet."

"I'm not sure if it has anything to do with anything. I wrote it all down just in case."

"Make me a copy, will you?"

"Sure, Ted. By the way, what did you find upstairs ...anything?"

The bathroom door opened. Ana asked, "Are you gentlemen sure about the coffee?"

"Yes, ma'am, said Don. We'll need your name, though. Who else lives here with you?"

"Just my son, Diego. He should be on his way from school. He'll be here soon."

"Ted reached for Don's watch. It's after three right now. I guess we might as well wait. Can I change my mind about that coffee, Lady?"

"Please, call me Ana. I'll get it for you. And what about you, Mister...?

"O'Brien! Sure, I'll have some, thanks."

Fifteen minutes later

(*Click*)

The door from the hallway opened.

"Hi Mom, there's a mess of cops out... Oh! I didn't know you had company?"

Ted stood and extended his hand. "Hi, I'm Detective Williams and this is my partner Detective O'Brien. We need to ask you a few questions."

"Sure, sir. What do you need to know?"

"Let's start with your name?"

"Diego Rivera."

"We need to know if you heard anything upstairs last night, like a door being broken into and if you were a friend of Joe Barnes?"

"No, not really. We never talked much. He never said hello, so…uh, I really can't say I know anything about him."

"Okay…and what about the noise last night. Hear anything?"

"Yes…but I was beat. I fell asleep on the couch watching Law Man. I thought it might be Joe fixing something up there."

"Is this where you usually sleep," Detective Williams asked, motioning toward the couch.

"Yes, but I always put a sheet down first. Last night I was so tired, I didn't even do that."

"I would think you could hear everything that goes on in that hall, you being this close to the door and all. What time was that about?"

"When I went to bed? Around eight thirty."

"So, then…you did hear banging upstairs?"

"Just that one time. Like I told you, I figured it was Joe. Before I knew it, I fell asleep like a rock."

"What about you, Ma'am, hear anything?"

"Yes! Maybe around nine? I didn't look. I was too tired."

"Not even a peek out of that window right there?" O'Brien asked.

"No, I stayed in bed."

Ted stood up from the chair. "I guess that wraps it up for now. Thanks for the coffee."

"Same here," said Don. "It's a little strong, but it's exactly what I needed. Oh, and Let me have your full names before we go…you know…for the record."

"Ana and Diego Rivera," Ana replied.

"No middle name for either of you?"

"Ana Lucia Robles Rosario Riv…"

"Whew! Give me a second while I write that all down. What was after Lucia?"

"R-o-b-l-e-s…R-o-s-a-r-i-o…R-i-v-e-r-a."

"Mine is Miguel, sir."

"Got it! Okay folks, have a good day. We'll keep in touch in case we need anything else."

"So long, officers," Diego said.

At the bottom of the stoop, Detective Williams stopped next to the patrolman guarding the front of the house from onlookers. "How long did they say you had to stay here?"

"Until you and forensics left, but not before I checked in with the sergeant."

"When you see him, let him know I'm coming right back to talk to the landlord. Is he home, by the way?"

"The guy in the basement? I ain't seen nobody come or go, except that kid that went in a couple of minutes ago."

"Okay, fine. Hey, it's cold out here. Why don't you go on up and wait in the hallway."

"Sarge told me to stay outside until he got back. He's probably gonna check up on me any minute."

"Williams read the name plate on his coat."

"Go on up, Nicholas."

"Nick, sir."

"It's okay, Nick. I'll cover for you. Tell him Detective Williams said it was okay."

"All right, Mr. Williams."

"I'll be right back. Ready, Don?"

The two detectives turned the corner toward Herzog's Deli.

"There's a phone right there," said Don. I'll make the call to the captain. You got any dimes on ya?"

Williams checked his pockets. "I'll get some change. As far as going back to the building, I think it's a waste o' time. None of those people had anything to do with it, and except for the lady upstairs, they all stayed nice and safe in their little rooms and not a peep out of any of them."

"We still gotta talk to the owner."

"You go ahead and check in, Don, I'll talk to the owner. Why don't you finish up on that assault case on Atlantic Avenue when you get back to headquarters and I'll catch up with you there. I noticed you like doing paper work."

"Very funny. Sure, that's fine with me. Hey, what about upstairs…the lady?"

"You'll hear it all when I get back. Don't worry, I'll give you some of the credit. Go ahead…start the call. I'll go in and get change."

Finished with his break inside D'avino's grocery, Bob Scanlon crossed the street to the front of Diego's building. "Hey Nick, you up there?"

"Right here," said Nick, emerging with a cup of coffee."

Joining him on the landing, Scanlon asked, "Hey…heard anything?"

"Yeah, and thanks for the coffee, Bob."

"I would o' got you some. Why didn't you say something when I passed by before, you rookie?"

"Forget it Bob, it's okay. I got this from the lady inside. What's up?"

"Did you hear anything? About upstairs, I mean?"

"Upstairs? Yeah, I did. The forensic guys were talking to the sarge earlier."

"Okay, so…what happened?"

"You heard about that guy they found dead in Central Park, right, the one that was murdered?"

Scanlon nodded. He was all ears.

"Well…his room is right up there."

"Hey, no shit!"

"Yeah, and they were saying that a bunch o' guys broke in last night and trashed the place looking for something."

"What do you suppose they were looking for?"

"The way the forensic guys were talking, it had to be really important, like a heck of a lot of money. That's all I know."

"Hey, here comes Williams. I gotta go. Hello, Ted, what's up?"

"Hey, Bob, is this your beat these days?"

"Yeah, why? Where the hell've you been? I had this beat for the last two years."

"Okay, okay, so don't get all huffy about it. Listen, do me a favor. Keep an eye on the building whenever you get on the block, alright? Ladies inside are all scared. Let them see you out front from time to time. You know, hang around a little bit if you can."

"Yeah, sure. Say, what gives with upstairs? There some kind o' hidden treasure up there?"

"Whatever it was, nobody found anything and they tore the place apart looking for it."

"What do you think they were looking for… money?" Scanlon asked.

"I don't know and I wouldn't tell you if I did. That answer your question?"

"Why? You know me!"

"And you know me and the system and how it works, right?"

"Sure, sure! Who gives a crap, anyway? See ya 'round the station."

Monday 6:21 P.M.
84th Precinct
Patrolmen's Locker Room

"Hey Scanlon, I heard the mob was lookin' for a bunch o' dough on your beat Saturday night?" a patrolman changing clothes asked.

"That ain't none of your business, turd ball," Scanlon retorted.

"Yeah, well, some o' da guys heard the captain and Williams talking."

"Oh? What'd they say?"

"Now I ain't tellin' you nuthin'."

"Hey, fuck you, Frankie. I already know about it, anyway."

"Maybe about dem being there, but not the rest of the story…and it's a real hum dinger."

"Okay, so ya got me! What'd ya hear?"

"This came down from my bother in-law in Manhattan, so keep it to yourself. He's a cop in the 18th, so I know it's the real deal."

"So, go ahead!"

"He was over my house last night, right? What he said was, Spillane's boys were looking for ten G's from that Barnes guy. He never paid any payments on the loan and the interest went through the roof."

"Okay, then they got the money?"

"Wait! Let me finish, will ya? They figured Barnes hid it in his room, that's why they came to Brooklyn Saturday."

"Then they found it?"

"Who the hell knows? Either they found the money and killed him anyway, or they got nothing and killed him because they were pissed off at him. Supposedly, Barnes gambles on the horses."

"He bets on horses?"

"The Trotters. The only thing is, nobody knows for sure if that's where the money went."

"Wow! You mean the dough could still be up there?"

Frankie shrugged. "Forensics searched the room and found nuthin'. Only thing is, there wasn't any stubs or anything to show he was anywhere around a race track recently."

Scanlon frowned. "Nah! There ain't nothin' up there."

"You gonna look?"

"Hell no! Number one, I don't breathe so good underwater. Number two, according to you, the mob already searched the place. And finally, number three, it's a bunch of malarkey. Your brother in law is jerkin' your pecker."

"Yeah, sure, you'll be up there soon enough, pulling every brick off that building."

"Not likely, turd ball. See ya later."

"Screw you, too, Scanlon."

Tuesday 9:05 A.M.

Ana unlocked the front door. "Hello officer."

Bob Scanlon made the greeting as short as possible. "Yeah! I gotta go up… close some loose ends up there."

"Can I make you some coffee?"

"Nah!"

"The man for the doors is upstairs."

"I know, I saw the truck outside. I gotta go!"

Scanlon climbed the steps to the noise of someone hammering on the top floor.

"You almost done up here?"

Val, from Valentine's Hardware, looked over his shoulder. "I'll be outa here in a sec. I gotta fix this door jamb and make a few adjustments."

Inside Mary's room, a milk box lay next to the wall alongside the door. She quietly slid it under her butt and stared through the key hole.

"Leave the door open when you're done," Scanlon added. "I have to finish my report and I don't want to forget anything. I…uh, I have to write a description of the rooms."

Val, a balding, bespectacled man of average height, squinted at the name plate. "Sure, officer…uh…Robert Scanlon. That 2B's unlocked if you want to go in? It's empty except for a few pieces of furniture. Cops took everything else out last night when I was here fixing that other door across the hall."

"The front door? Who went in there, the cops?"

"I dunno! Somebody broke in over the weekend. What a job that was. Broke the whole damn catch mechanism. I had to move the lock farther up to get enough wood to work with. Some lady lives in there."

"A lady?"

"Yeah, she's in there right now."

"Is that right?"

"I'm almost finished with this back room."

"Don't forget to leave it open."

Scanlon entered room 2B, closed the door and looked around. He pulled the string to a bare 60 watt bulb hanging from a loose fixture in the ceiling. The drawers in the bureau were neatly tucked in place. He removed each of them completely where he knew people liked to hide money in an envelope scotch taped to the undersides or to the back of the shelves. The bureau itself, he laid on its side to check the bottom.

There were no cuts in the mattress and nothing behind the radiator or underneath it, 'though those would have been the first places anyone would have checked. The closet appeared clean, the floor boards and molding there as well as in the rest of the room showed no signs of having been tampered with.

He entered the bathroom and thoroughly checked there as well. When he was done, he stood in the middle of the hall. "You almost done?"

"Yup!" Val replied. "I have to get the last of my tools together."

A few minutes later, Scanlon heard the tool box shut.

"See ya," the maintenance man said.

The cop ignored his departure while steadily focusing on the roof hatch, his arms folded across his chest. After a search of the back room proved fruitless, he returned to the street.

Inside 2A, Mary backed away from the key hole, left the TV on and settled into the recliner.

Chapter Six
The Steel Box

"I'm doing things differently with the team this year," Larry said to Diego.

"What's going to be different from last year, Larr?"

"I'm gonna practice."

"You? Practice?"

"Yeah, why? Ya don't believe me?"

Diego tried his best to look sincere. "Sure I do. We need another good player."

"I don't wanna sit around this time. I wanna play first base."

"Hey, that's great, but you'll need a lot of practice for that."

"I'm gonna hit, too. You know, like Jose, but I need you to show me?"

"I can't teach you what I can't do myself. I'll tell you what. I'll check the roof for a decent ball and if I find one, we'll go to the school yard and practice hitting. I got one from the garbage men, but it's kind of new. I'm saving it for the team this spring."

Larry's eyes brightened. "Good idea. Let's go up!"

"Stay down here. I'll give you a yell if I find one and throw it to you."

"Why can't I go with you?"

"Because I'm not supposed to be up there in the first place. Wait down here, I'll be right back."

At the top floor, a wrought iron ladder lead to the roof hatch. Diego unlatched both eyehooks, pushed the cover off and set it to the side.

Searching his, as well as the adjoining roofs, he made his way to as far as Leroy's building before finding three pinkies and all them looking worn. He bounced each of them several times before settling on two. The dead ball, he leaned way back and tried to make a roof on the other side of the back yards. It sailed across the open space and hit one of the top floors and bounced into a yard below.

Back at the front edge of his own roof, he leaned over and yelled out to Larry. "I found two! You ready?"

"Go ahead…throw them down!"

The balls were dropped one at a time and right after that, Scanlon walked by from underneath an overhanging branch of a large maple.

"What're you doin' up there? Get off that roof!"

"Sorry officer. I'll come down right now."

"You better! And I don't want to see you up there again."

"Yes, sir."

"Asshole, Puerto Rican!" Scanlon muttered.

Diego watched the cop cross the street and then walk around the corner toward Bergen.

"I'll be right down, Larr!"

"Yeah, hurry up. I'll play stoop ball until you get here."

The roof was one of Diego's favorite places. He liked going up there, especially on a warm summer's night, though now, during December, it was chilly. He crossed to the back edge of the building and peered down into the yards, a few with dogs barking up at him. Clothes hung from lines strung from fire escapes to metal poles. Someone's pigeon coup, a homemade affair using scrap 2X4's and chicken wire, sat on the roof of the same building where he had thrown the ball. Weekends, the owner, with the aid of a long pole, could be seen training the birds to fly in a hovering circle above the coup. Diego would watch for hours as the birds swooped and dived and circled obediently.

Sitting with his back against the brick chimney of the building next door, he stared across the flatness of black tar paper on the roof of his own building, to the top floors of his old elementary school, P.S. 47, on the next block. He thought back to the fun he had had in sixth grade and Mrs. Oberdorfer and how he was sure she was in love with his father. Back then, she seemed quite adept at conjuring up any excuse she could think of to get him to pay her a visit. She would write Diego up for inattentiveness or arguing in class---whatever would work. She was awfully hard to look at, though. The kids even had a nickname for her, Mrs. Ed, a reference to the TV sit com, Mr. Ed, the talking horse.

Diego's gaze wandered downward to the chimney of his own building, recalling when he first moved to Brooklyn from Rochester. At the time it was a whole new adventure for him. The idea of living in a big city had intrigued him and he remembered being excited about the move.

As he pictured those early days, he noticed something amiss with the chimney of his own building. Something wasn't right. His head tilted to the side as he stared at it until he realized what it was. One of the capstones was ajar and slightly out of place with the rest. He got up to straighten it out, curious as to why there was no mortar holding the rectangular shaped stone securely in place.

Just like the rest of this building. The whole place is falling apart.

He slid the heavy stone ever so slightly so that it lined up with the ones next to it, leaned over and looked inside the shaft.

The deep, black depths of the bottomless chasm beckoned like a brick walled passageway to a dragon's lair. Diego, replete in knight's armor, peered into the darkness with sword drawn and glistening shield before him. He could hear the very breath of the hidden beast as it sounded from below. It bellowed up forcefully like a frightening nightmare, exuding smoke and cinders along with a rumbling that shook from the deepest depths---the castle keep in the far below.

The brave knight dared to grab the dragon by the tail.

Diego held onto the rope hanging downward inside the chimney and immediately felt the weight of something heavy tied to it. He pulled five feet of the rope up, hand-over-hand and retrieved a grey, steel container, similar in size to a cigar box. Curious, he laid it on top of the chimney, undid the latch and flipped the lid open.

Inside, was tucked a brick sized package wrapped tightly in brown paper. He carefully peeled it back from the corner and what he saw underneath gave him an instant feeling of elation. A nervous tingle ran down the length of his spine as he eyed a four inch stack of crisp new bills. On top, a portrait of Secretary of the Treasury, Alexander Hamilton, the only portrait on an American bill that faces left, seemed to smile back at him like an all knowing custodian. A keeper of riches and all that runs deep of meaningful virtues and the most moral of reaches, thanks to the artful brush strokes of John Trumball.

Diego thought to give the money to the police. They would know what to do with it. That would certainly be the right thing to do.

And then, thoughts of his mother, a new dress, a well-respected doctor for her, a home of their very own and all the Louie Armstrong records she could ever want to dance to, came immediately to mind. Could that be considered greed? Diego wasn't sure. And had he lifted the heavy capstone, instead of sliding it into position like he had done, both, the weighted rope and the steel box would have plunged three floors to the basement and into the fiery furnace.

Closing the lid, he flipped the latch, placed the end of the rope under the capstone and carefully lowered the box down the chimney. After a quick pit stop to the bathroom, he returned to the street with an aura of well-being and an immense feeling of wealth. As if nothing had happened, he met up with Larry.

"Where've you been?" his friend asked.

"The bathroom, let's go practice."

All day in school, on Wednesday, Diego thought of nothing else but the box full of money. His imagination went wild with thoughts of movies, trips to the Empire State Building, the Statue of Liberty and the Staten Island Ferry. He'd rent the whole damn boat and invite everyone on the block, everyone on Mr. Jackson's block and Louie's, too.

In time, he realized how foolish those thoughts were. And what if only that top bill was a ten? The rest could be all ones, or Monopoly Money for that matter. The new worry plagued him. He had to look again, count it, see how much was really there. He couldn't get any of it out of his mind.

3:06 P.M.

"Hi Mom, anything to eat?"

"Rice with eggs, and I made Jell-O for you, the green kind you like. How was school?"

"Okay, I guess. I'm starved!" Diego ate faster than usual.

"You're going to choke like that, slow down."

"I have to go up to the roof to look for more balls."

"So, what's the rush? Those balls aren't going anywhere."

"Yeah, I know."

"When you go upstairs, ask Maria if she needs something from the store."

Perfect! That's my excuse for going up there for nosy-body Mary...and Karen's kids, in case they see me going up there, too.

After a quick trip to the store and back, and knowing Mary would be busy stuffing her gizzards with two pounds of baked macaroni, a quart of chocolate milk and enough Twinkies to build Barbie a three story doll house, he silently climbed the ladder to the roof hatch. He had purposefully left the eyehooks off the last time to minimize noise the next time he went up. All he had to do was lift it and gently place it off to the side. He retrieved the steel box and opened it on top of the chimney. Removing the stack of bills, he sat with his back against the bricks of the chimney, thankful for the lack of wind. He removed the brown paper completely and thumbed the side of the bills to scroll through for a quick look.

All tens!

Double checking, he did it again and then divided the stack into two halves. He proceeded to count both of them three times each.

He couldn't believe it. He counted it again.

Ten thousand, and all in tens.

He now knew what it felt like to hold $10,000 dollars in his hands. Except for the five tens he put in his pocket, he wrapped it all up in the brown paper and placed it into the box with the lid closed shut.

Leaving the box lying on the floor of the roof, he stepped back toward the front of the building. There, he stared at the steel as if it was Black Beard's treasure chest resting half buried somewhere on a beach in the outer banks of North Carolina.

He dug his toes into warm, gritty sand. Before him, and in audience, lay the vast and open sea. There, the parallel rays of a setting sun burned as would rubescent flames across a rolling, copen surf.

Was this enough money to buy the D'avino's store, he wondered, or that fancy, Ford station wagon with the wooden sides parked across the street? Maybe Herzog would sell him the deli or maybe he would just buy the whole damn block for that matter. He could probably buy a city bus, or a taxi or maybe even ten taxis?

Ten thousand dollars. Ten thousand dollars.

He kept repeating that to himself.

With his arms folded across his chest, Scanlon continued to eye what he could see of Diego's head moving about the front of the roof. And not that he totally believed it, or could even count that high, but if he put two and two together, there was a remote possibility that the kid knew something. He had never considered the roof, but why not? As far as he knew, it was the only place nobody looked. Still, the whole idea seemed doubtful and right now he had more pressing things to do with his time.

After dinner, Ana took her usual long shower. Diego seized the moment to go into her bedroom. He reached inside the closet and picked up a pair of her best dress shoes. The heels looked worn and the black finish as dull as worn asphalt. A decorative leather bow on the left shoe barely hung there with a push pin and precariously leaned at an odd angle to that of the right. He memorized the size, 6M, and moved on to her favorite dress at the end of the rack on the only wooden hanger in the closet. One of only three dresses, the other two were well worn, one of which had missing buttons, the other, a zipper that didn't work. Diego read the tag on Ana's favorite dress, size 7 Petit.

At Larry's building, he rang the doorbell.

"Hello Diego…you looking for Larry?"

"Hi, Mrs. Constantine. Yes. Is he home?"

"Just a minute. He's right here."

Larry beamed. "Hey, what's up, Diego?"

"Nothing much! I'm going downtown to buy my mother a present. You want to go?"

"Downtown? Sure!"

"I found fifty dollars and I want to get her something."

"Fifty dollars! **Holy Murgatroyd!** Where?"

"Uh…In a hole!"

"In a hole? Where?"

"I can't tell you. I mean…that's all that was in there, fifty dollars. That was it!"

"Damn! How come I never find anything like that?"

"Are you coming or not?"

"Yeah, but let's go to the movies, instead. *The Commancheros* with John Wayne is playing at the Majestic. We even got enough to go to Woolworth's for banana splits. Come on, man! Whaddya say?"

"Larry, is that all you think about…food?"

"Yeah, of course! So, whaddya say?"

"I'll tell you what. After we're done we'll get ice cream, all right?"

"Oh, I guess so, but I gotta square it with my mom first."

May's Department Store
Fulton Street

"Man, this is embarrassing," said Larry, upon entering the women's section on the second floor. "What're we getting up here, by the way?"

"Buying a dress."

"A dress? In front of all these people?"

"So! We're not going to see these people anymore, what's it matter?"

"Hey, that girl's looking at us."

"No she's not. Stop the bullshit and help me."

Larry clenched his teeth. **"Help you what! Find a dress?** I'm not doin' that! Besides, I don't know nothin' 'bout no dresses."

"If you see something that looks nice, let me know, that's all."

"What a **freakin'** waste of my time. **Fine**…don't say it! I'll look."

"How's this one?" said Diego, pulling a black dress with a wide, white lacy collar off the rack."

"If she's not a nun, put it back."

"Okay, is this one any better, its kind o' nice?"

"What's with the puffy sleeves, she goin' parachutin' somewhere?"

"Very funny! Are you going to get serious and help me, or not?"

While Diego continued the search, Larry checked from the other end of the long line of dresses. He soon found one he actually liked and held it above the rack.

"Hey, this looks pretty good."

Diego glared at him with a distrusting eye.

"No, really, I really mean it this time."

"Let me see it!" Diego took the dress from him and held it up against the boy's chest."

"Hey! What the hell are you doing? You want all these girls to see us."

"I hate to be the one to tell you this, Larr, but I think they already have? Besides, they're leaving."

"Well…at least you didn't have to wave a flag at them."

"Shut up and hold still." Diego held the dress up next to Larry. "You're about the right height."

"Right height? Right height for **what,** Diego?"

"To try this on."

"**What!** What're you nuts? I'm not trying nothing on!"

"Hey, just imagine a delicious banana split, with all those strawberries and chocolaty syrup just oozing over the…"

"Shut up, Diego?"

"So go! Try it on before someone comes. There's nobody in that dressing room. Hurry up! Go and try it on so we can go!"

"Whaddya mean, **that dressing room**. I never said I was trying anything on. You go! It's your mother!"

"Choclatee, syrupee, yummy strawber…"

"You know? You really suck sometimes, Diego. Give me that!" Larry snatched the dress from him. "And if you see any girls around, you better tell me before I come out."

"Thanks heaps, Larr."

"You're not welcome. We're doing this fast, and when we're done with this crap, don't forget you're buying me a banana split, and it better be a big one for this bullshit."

He entered the last dressing room at the far end and hastily put the dress over his head. He got his arms through and struggled to pull it down from the sides, but couldn't get the waist line past his upper chest. Poking his head around the curtain with his arms stuck above the top of the dress, he checked both ways before stepping out. "Look at this shit! Are you satisfied, now, you fuckin' Puerto Rican?"

They both laughed heartily at that, Larry more than Diego did.

"Wait there while I get you another one."

"One more, Diego, that's it and then we're leaving!"

Diego returned with the same style, red dress, a size 16 Petit. "Here, try this on."

"Yeah, right! This is it! Gimme that!" Larry snatched the dress out of his hands.

Shortly, he slapped the curtain to the side and after a quick check, stepped out. "Well? Yes or no? Hurry up…quick!"

"You didn't take your pants off."

"**What!** I ain't gonna do that! Hurry up! Do you like it, or not?"

"On you, sweetie? Not really," Diego laughed.

Larry took a step backward, stiffened his lips, and in a low, raspy tone, said, "Hey, screw you, pal. Now I ain't doin' this no more!"

"That's fine! You'll see!"

"Whaddya mean, I'll see? What 're you gonna do?"

"Oh...you'll see!"

"Come on Diego. Don't be that way."

"You know what Larr, I had a surprise for you, but now I don't think I'm going to give it to you anymore."

"Aw man, you see that shit? Now why do you gotta be that way. Okay, fine, I'll try on one more dress, but **that's** it."

"Without the pants."

"Man, do I really have to?"

"If you want the surprise, yes."

"Why does life have to be so hard? So where's the damn dress?"

"Hang on, and stop cursing. I left it over there."

In a rush to get the whole thing over with, and forgetting for the moment that he was still wearing a dress, Larry followed Diego to the opposite end of the rack.

"Oh, crap! Why didn't you tell me I still had this stupid dress on?"

"Stop cursing, will you?"

Larry quickly pulled the dress over his head and flung it high into the air toward the other side of the rack."

"Here, try this red one on. I saw it before when you were in there changing."

Larry reluctantly snatched it from him and without another word, shuffled towards the dressing room, dragging the dress along the floor behind him.

Two aisles over, Butchie's mother lay a second blouse over her arm. She was now heading between the dress racks to the checkout with her son.

"Hey, Diego. What're you doin' here?"

"Butchie! Oh...uh...I'm with my mother. She's trying something on."

"Oh, yeah...well, hey, this is my mother."

"Hi, ma'am, I'm pleased to..."

The heavy curtain to the dressing room suddenly swung to the side with Larry looking down and brushing the front of the dress flat. "This better be it, because I...I... **oh, crap!"**

Opened mouthed and wide eyed, Larry melted where he stood, in the middle of the aisle with a sickening feeling welling up inside his stomach. The dress fit perfectly with Larry's chubby knees barely showing below the hem line, his red cheeks matching the dress to a T.

"Well, well," Butchie slowly said. Covering his mouth, he suddenly exploded in laughter. As soon as he was able to, he quipped, "Hi there, Mrs. Rivera, so pleased to meet you."

"Come on Butchie! Let's get out of here!" his mother barked.

Larry said nothing else. Totally defeated, his arms were left hanging loosely at the sides of the dress, his head hanging as low as he felt inside. Turning quietly around, his heels scuffed the floor as he shuffled his way back to the dressing room, his short and chubby, powder white legs, fully exposed beneath the dress.

And Diego never even liked that dress, nor any of the other ones Larry had tried on. It was all in jest and he enjoyed every minute of it. He pulled the one he had set aside from the rack, a dress he had already picked out the first time his friend stepped into the dressing room. It was a red dress of a totally different style, size 7 petit.

After an appeasement of not one, but two banana splits, Larry exited Woolworth holding his belly, 'less it fell to his knees. With a satisfied look on his face, he licked the chocolate from the corner of his mouth and headed with Diego to Baker's Shoes on the next block. Spared from trying on anything else, Larry found out what the surprise was; nothing---nada---zilch, and it pissed him off for being had so easily.

When Diego got home, he laid the shopping bags on the kitchen table and sat with anticipation.

"Diego, what is all this?" asked Ana, as she rummaged through the bags.

"I'm taking you to church tomorrow. It's been a while and I know you would like to go."

"Yes, a long time. Where did you get all of this stuff? How much did you spend?"

"Mom, don't worry about any of that? I found some money, that's all."

"Oh, my goodness! You found money? Where?"

"In the street. It was laying in the gutter."

"In the street? Maybe somebody is looking for this money?"

"I don't think so. I waited around for a while, but nobody came by. Go ahead, Mom, take a look inside."

Ana removed the dress from the bag, held it up and sighed with a beginning of tears. "Look at this dress. It's so pretty." (*Sniff!*) "Fourteen, ninety eight? So much money! We could have bought food with this money."

"I got you shoes to go along with it and a pair of stockings."

Ana reached into the other bag and placed the shoe box on the table. She wiped her eyes and opened the box carefully as if any sudden movement would make it all disappear. Unfolding the paper wrapping carefully to the sides, she took out one of the shoes.

Diego mirrored her smile. "They looked like the shoes in the closet, the ones you used to wear when you dressed up. I was lucky, they still had the same style, so I bought them. How do you like them, Mom?"

Ana stood there shaking. She leaned forward and kissed her son on the cheek.

"You made your momma very happy, Diego."

Sunday Morning

"You're going to look beautiful," said Karen, finishing with Ana's eye liner. "How does she look, Diego?"

"Wow, Mom! You look so pretty. I really mean it."

"Stand up for a second so I can fix your stockings," said Karen.

Ana checked her makeup in a handheld mirror while Karen straightened the hems of the stockings so that the thick black lines ran down the exact middle of the back of her legs.

"You have dancer's legs," said Karen.

"Gracias! I used to be strong. I danced a lot."

"Go ahead and sit and I'll put your shoes on."

"Mom, I can't believe how pretty you look in that dress."

"What do you mean you can't believe it?" said Karen. "She was always pretty."

"Well, yeah I know, but you know what I mean?"

"Of course I do. I'm only kidding, can't you tell?"

Diego headed for the door. "I think I better get over to Atlantic Avenue and hail a cab. I want mom to get the best seat in church."

Ana blew her son a kiss. "I'm so lucky to have you as a son."

As soon as the taxi pulled in front of the house, Diego ran down and opened the cab door.

"How come you don't have your coat on?" he asked Ana, upon seeing her at the top of the stoop.

"It's too ugly to put over this pretty dress. I have this instead." Ana closed a black, lace shawl around her shoulders.

"It's cold out. I'll get your coat."

He returned and held it open. An overall brown color, speckled with red, yellow, and white dots, the outside of the right pocket was torn with half of it hanging down the side. The bottom button was missing, leaving a tuft of brown threads.

"I cannot find the opening," Ana said. She continued to feel around for the sleeve through the tattered lining. "I always wanted to fix this stupid coat, but I keep forgetting to send you to buy the right color thread."

She adjusted the coat around her shoulders before fastening the buttons. "If I knew I was going to church…"

Karen said. "Don't worry, Ana, it doesn't look that bad. I'll help you down the steps."

Arriving at church by 10:50, Diego and another parishioner assisted Ana up the stone steps to the double doors where the last of the nine o'clock faithful were still exiting. She immediately took off the coat, stuck it under her arm and entered the first pew before the altar. The coat, she left folded on the bench and adjusted the shawl over her full breast before sitting down.

Nudges from attentive wives turned their men's focus away from her and back to the front. The rest of the church soon filled with every seat taken and the back entryways starting to crowd with late standees. Bob Scanlon and his wife sat in the row opposite Ana's, and he had noticed.

Fifteen minutes before the end of the service, Diego walked three blocks up Court Street to hail a cab on Atlantic Avenue.

Outside, four men stood on all sides of Ana with offers to assist her down the church steps to the sidewalk. It took two more to hold the taxi door open.

"Why didn't you put the coat on?" said Diego.

"It's not that cold," Ana said.

"She'll be all right," said a man holding her gently by the hand.

At the top of the steps, Scanlon watched as she entered the taxi cab.

"Are you coming?" his impatient wife asked.

"I'll be right there. Don't worry about me! Go on, what're ya waitin' for? I'll catch up!" He folded his arms in front of him. "Look at them two," he muttered, to no one but himself, his head shaking subtly from side to side.

"Court and Carol," Diego said to the driver.

The taxi zipped straight down Court Street and in less than six minutes, pulled in front of Anthony's Pizzeria.

Ana sat up straight and peered out of the window. "What are we doing here?"

"Come on, Mom, I'm treating you to lunch."

Excited for the rare treat, Ana couldn't believe all that was happening. "Oh, my goodness! Thank you, Diego."

"Don't worry about getting home, either. I have enough."

Ana entered the pizzeria and laid her coat across her lap as she slid into a booth next to a window. The torn linings, she stuck inside the sleeves. "This is the best day I've had in a long time. No rain, I went to church, we took a taxi, and now you are buying me pizza."

The kitchen door to the restaurant swung open. "Diego! Slap me five, man."

"Hey, Louis. How's everything?"

"Good! Long time no see."

"This is my mother."

"Hi, ma 'me." Impressed, Louis asked, "What can I get you folks?

"A large pizza, two Cokes and some zeppolis."

"You got it! I'll be right back."

"Well, Mom, are you havin' fun?"

"I love this. So you were here before?"

This is the place I told you about. Remember last summer when me and Mr. Jackson and Larry and the guys all went to the pier?"

"Yes, when Louie chased those bad boys away. I remember what you told to me."

"Right, well, we came here a few times after that day."

The door to the kitchen opened and this time it was Anthony. He came out carrying their plate of zeppolis and two sodas. "Looka who we gotta here... Mr. a Diego. And who's a this a beauty?"

"Hi Anthony, this is my mother."

"So young and with a face like a the angels. That's a fine a boy you gotta there."

"Thank you," said Ana.

Anthony sat with them and reiterated the story about the gang of kids that had given Diego and his friends so much trouble. "Nunzio, heeza eena the Brookaleen detention."

"The Atlantic Avenue Jail? What for?"

"Stealeen the cars. He's a big athief, thata boy."

After finishing most of the pizza and getting ready to find a cab, Diego took a quick glance out of the window where he saw Louie approaching the pizzeria.

As soon as Louie entered the restaurant, he scanned the room. "There you are!"

"Louie! What a surprise," said Diego.

Louie said, "Ant'ney called me and told me you wuz in here."

"By the way, this is my mom, Ana."

"Hello, Ana." Louie took a second, long look at her. "Wow, now dats a plate o' meatballs. Ana, you look like a queen!"

Ana blushed.

From behind Louie, a tall man around Ana's age stepped forward.

Louie said, "This is my older brother, Danny. He ain't neva been married 'cuz he been too busy playin' in traffic."

"Hi, Ana. Nice to meet you," said Danny.

Ana looked back flirtatiously, 'though with a hint of shyness. "So why are you playing in traffic, Danny?"

"I'm a bus driver."

The get together lasted for over an hour. When Louie got up to play records on the juke box, Diego took the opportunity to use the rest room. Ana found herself alone with Danny.

"So, why haven't you gotten married?" She asked.

"I never met the right one."

"Not even to give someone a ring?"

"Yeah, I got close a few times, but you know how it is. We bus drivers work crazy shifts…weekends, holidays. It can be stressful at times in a relationship. Who's gonna put up with that?"

"That's too bad."

"I was with the last girl for seven years. I really thought she was the right one, but she walked out on me. She hated my hours. Heck, I only have another five years to go for my pension."

"Five years? Arent' you a little young for retirement? What would you do?"

"Move! I've been thinkin'…maybe to the island. It's quieter out there. I thought I'd take the test for the Post Office…get another pension going. At least they have regular hours and I'll still be outside. It'll be good for me to walk a little after so many years behind the wheel."

"I can understand that, Danny."

The table filled again as everyone returned to their seats. After the music selections played themselves out, everyone exchanged goodbyes. Danny gave Ana and Diego a ride home.

***

"Can I make you coffee, Danny?"

"I have to go in early tomorrow and need to get some sleep. Coffee keeps me awake. But thanks anyway."

As he left, he shook hands with Diego before stepping through the outside door. Addressing Ana, he said, "I'm glad I met the both of you today."

Ana smiled sweetly from her apartment doorway. "Bye, Danny."

"I'll walk you outside," said Diego.

Danny stepped down the first two steps, still searching for the words he could have said to Ana, 'though his mind was still a horrible blank. He said goodbye again to Diego and took another four steps down before turning around with a thought.

"Say, would you mind if I go back in for a second to ask your mother if she could go to a wedding with me?"

Diego looked at him with an all knowing grin. "Not at all, Danny. I think she would really like that."

Monday afternoon

Standing in front of D'avino's, Scanlon eyed the open door to 240 Dean Street, left ajar by Karen's two girls.

There's something on that roof that has been interesting that kid. Not only that, he and his mother sure seem to be spending a lot of money, lately.

His watch read 2:47. He crossed the street, entered Diego's building and hustled to the top floor, the heavy footsteps, alerting Mary to the keyhole.

The heavy steps continued as the cop walked down the hall toward her door, and then the reverberating sound of size twelve shoes hitting metal as the cop purposefully climbed the steel ladder.

Relieved to see that it was only a cop, Mary settled into the easy chair and as usual, dozed with the TV left on.

Fifteen minutes later, Diego closed the outside door and entered his apartment. "Hi, Mom!"

"How was school?"

"Okay…pretty good, actually."

"Are you hungry?"

"Not right now."

In her usual Spanish accent, she said, "You should eat. It is not good to go all day without eating something. I can make you a hamburger and fresh fries… or maybe some…"

"Mom…Mom, hold on a second. First of all, they're not called fresh fries…they're French fries. Never mind, forget that! I've been thinking. I need to tell you something really important."

"Important? What is it, Diego? You look troubled."

"You better sit on the couch. This is big. A real lulu."

"A le lo li?"

"No, no…it's…it's not about that island music."

"My goodness. What's the matter?"

"It's nothing bad. It's about the money I found."

"The fifty dollars? I know. It's all gone. Don't worry about that."

"No, Mom. I didn't tell you the whole story."

Ana read the worry on Diego's face. As they both sat on the couch, she reached for his hand and with surety and a consoling tone, said, "Whatever it is, we can fix it."

"Mom, it's nothing like that. It's kind of good actually."

She sat up and attentively focused on her son.

"Okay…look…it's this way. You remember when I found the money, right?"

"Si, of course."

"Well…it wasn't fifty dollars."

"Oh?" Ana straightened in her chair.

Diego took a deep breath, looked into her attentive, brown eyes, and with reserve, softly said, "It was ten thousand dollars."

Speechless, Ana's lower jaw dropped. Her eyes opened wide and then she sank into the sofa. "Ten-thousand dollars? Oh my goodness!" Covering her mouth, she gasped through her spread out fingers.

"Take it easy, Mom, it's all there."

Ana bolted upright. She did her best to quickly calm herself and then said, "So…where is, **there**?"

"The roof!" Diego casually answered.

"Here? This roof? This roof up here?" Her forefinger was left pointing at the ceiling.

Diego quietly nodded.

Turning from him, she thought long and hard. "This is bad money. It's the money everybody is looking for."

"I know, but that's over. Nobody knows about it but me."

Shaking her head, Ana said nothing else. She remained silent while contemplating about what to do.

"Mom?"

"No! I'm thinking!"

Her son waited with a held breath.

"Did you tell this to any of your friends?" she asked.

"No, nobody."

"Not to Mister Jackson?"

"Nope!"

"Not even to your friend, Larry?"

"Nope, not even Larry."

Ana continued to think for a long time, a very long time. She then finally said, "Go get the money and bring it here. We're going to keep this quiet for now."

"I was considering giving it to the police."

Smiling dismissively at her son, she shook her head and said, "Give it to the police? No, no, no! They will have a big party with that money. Go up there and get it. We will do nothing else until we think about this."

Relieved, Diego left for the top floor. He silently passed 2A, with Mary's snores reverberating on the other side of the door. He climbed the ladder, pushed the lid quietly to the side and stepped onto the roof. Alongside the chimney, he stood motionless for a moment, grinning while staring at the capstone with a thought of his mother's face when he finally put the money in her hands.

"So...now we're going to find out what was so interesting up here... right, kid?"

Diego's head jerked around just as Scanlon stepped from behind the chimney of the connecting roof next door. Seeing the uniformed cop, he moved away from the brick chimney and stepped toward the back of the building.

"Well, now...so what have you been doing up here? Huh, kid?"

"N...nothing, looking for pinky balls, that's all!"

"Pinky balls? Oh, you mean those little rubber balls?"

"Y-Yes. We keep losing them and they're always getting hit up here."

"Oh! Right, right, right! So that's the reason I always see you up here?"

"Yes, officer."

With a soft and sympathetic voice, Scanlon added, "I see. Okay, that's all I wanted to know."

The cop casually approached and put an arm around the boy's shoulders. Ya see...I've been up here lookin' around for a while. Funny...I didn't see any balls anywhere up here. In fact, the roof is as clean as a whistle."

In the next instant, Scanlon punched Diego in the stomach so hard it knocked the wind out of him. The boy doubled over and sank to his knees.

Standing over him with disdain, the cop said, "Ya see kid, I can hurt ya where nobody would ever notice it. I ain't playin' with you no more, I know you found the money and I want it. Right now!"

"I don't know what you're talkin' about." Diego gritted his teeth and clutched his stomach.

"You know exactly what I'm talkin' about. Now, stand up."

Diego gradually got to his feet, and not one step from the edge of the roof. He didn't realize he was doing it, but his gaze kept shifting back and forth from the cop to the chimney.

"What are you lookin' at?" Scanlon forcefully yelled.

He scoured the roof, staring with inquisitive, glaring eyes. Turning back to the boy and then to the chimney, he saw nothing amiss other than the opened hatchway.

"Stay right there! Don't move!"

As the cop neared the chimney, he continually turned to look scornfully at Diego. He searched behind it and the area immediately around the chimney. "What's over here, you little spic bastard. You better tell me or I'll break every fuckin' bone in your body. You hear me?"

Diego, nurtured in obedience, didn't budge. All he could do was hope that the cop didn't look inside.

Returning to it, Scanlon tapped the outside for loose bricks, all the while watching Diego for a reaction. When he reached the top, the boy twitched and nervously looked away.

"Whoops! Huh? Did you say something?" The cop's thin lips stretched into a grin. He felt along the cold surface of the capstones, turned toward the boy and snapped, "It's here somewhere, isn't it?"

Leaning over the chimney on his forearms, he looked down the dark shaft, leaned a little more forward and then burst out laughing. "Well, well, well...what do we have here?"

Scanlon's voice echoed from the deep depths as if it had come from a cavern somewhere within the bowls of the earth. Reaching in, he pulled up on the rope and grabbed the steel box with one hand while removing the capstone with the other. His joy suddenly turned to anger as soon as he looked back at Diego—a boy whose lowered gaze stared nervously at the dust-filled blackness of the tar roof.

"My, my...I wonder what this could be?" Scanlon dropped the capstone next to Diego's feet. He opened the steel box and unraveled the brown paper. "Well I'll be!" The cop's overly stretched grin returned.

Fingering the bills, he knew immediately that it had to be the money the mob was missing, 'though hiding the find from them and everyone else would be another matter. Who, besides the kid knew it was here? His mother? His fat, chubby friend? Or...perhaps both of them? The thought troubled him.

"You know what? I knew there was something up with you when I saw you and your mother in church yesterday. Been spending this money, huh?"

He slammed the metal lid closed and set it down on the roof, not far from the capstone. Scowling, he glared at the boy, a boy who was still looking downward without knowing what was to come next.

The cop growled under his breath. What he saw was neither a boy, nor innocence, but only an object that stood in his way; an insignificant nothing of little worth.

"You little prick!" He sneered.

There was no other way, he thought. He had to get rid of the problem.

Afraid to get hit again, Diego squatted low and covered his head from the blows he knew would come raining down at any moment. He clamped his eyes shut, his mind completely void of anything other than the pain he would soon have to endure from the cop's pounding fist.

"You little son of a bitch! You thought you were going to keep all of this money, didn't you, you little bastard. Who the hell do you think you are that you should take it all for yourself?"

Emboldened by his own words, the cop's heart began to race from the thought of what he knew had to be done. He backed away a few steps and turned toward the front of the building.

As hard a man as Scanlon thought himself to be, and was, doing the inevitable would be no easy task. He faced the boy once more, ready to put an end to the whole inconvenience. Stepping quickly forward, his right shoe came down on the sharp corner of the steel box.

Diego jumped to the side as the cop stumbled toward him. At that same moment, Scanlon's left shoe stepped on the end of the capstone. His ankle twisted precariously, and 'though he tried to regain his balance, the forward momentum forced him over the edge.

Scanlon's basso, resonant scream lasted a full second and a half. His neck hit the chain link fence three stories below, severing his head from his blue uniformed body. The body landed in the landlord's tomato patch while the head fell into the yard next door. It rolled with a spray of blood across a stone patio, sending the neighbor's German shepherd to the far corner of the yard with its tail between its legs.

Opening his eyes, Diego stared past his feet into the yard three floors down. The horror of what had just happened frightened him so much, he froze there for a long while, unable to move. He glared intensely at the body dressed in blue, headless and lying within the remnant, grey stubbles of the tomato plants. The sight sickened him. He checked across the yards to the back of the houses on the other side and at the only windows he could see. Hearing nothing and seeing no one, he picked up the box and headed for the opened hatchway.

Mary!

He couldn't go back the way he had come. He had to think. There was another way down. He used it before when playing ring 'o levio, a hide and seek game that utilized the entire block as a playing field. And like that game, he crossed every roof on the block toward Bond Street. There, he climbed down a fire escape into someone's yard, jumped a fence and continued unhurried through an empty lot to the street as if nothing had happened.

Larry answered the bell to his apartment.

"Diego! Whassup, Pal?"

"Hey man, I never thought I'd be this happy to see you."

"What? What did you say?"

"Um, nothing Larr. You mind if I hang out for a little while?"

"Of course not. Say...you're sweating bullets. Are you okay?"

"Yeah, sure. I'm all right. This jacket's too warm, that's all. I'll take it off."

"I'm watchin' Roy Rogers."

"Sounds good."

"What's in the box, Dieg."

"Um...nothing! My diary, why?"

"So, why are you carrying a diary around?"

"In case I want to add something important."

"Oh! What're you writin' about?"

"Me! What else! It's a diary."

"Oh, yeah, that's right. But what's it say?"

"I can't tell you. A diary is supposed to be private."

"Yeah, I guess so...sorry."

6:32 P.M. 240 Dean Street
The Front Stoop

"Who called this in?" said Detective Williams to O'Brien.

"Some lady removing clothes from her line. She said she thought it was some of her clothes, you know, blown off the line by the wind? She freaked out when she took a closer look over the fence and saw Scanlon's body lying there without a head."

"I'd be shocked, too. Where did you find the head?"

"The dog! He was chewing on it by the back fence. Our guys nearly had to shoot the damn thing in order to get it away from him."

"Here we go again. You take downstairs, Don, and I'll see if Mary saw anything. You bring pictures?"

"Yes, but I only have one set."

"Let me show them to Mary so I don't have to go up these stairs any more than I have to."

"Sure! What's in the bag?"

Ted opened a brown paper bag and showed him the packages of Twinkies crowded inside. "Don't ask!"

"I won't."

Inside Mary's room, Ted handed the bag to her. "I brought you these."

Mary opened it and looked in. "Thank you, detective. I heard about the cop they found in the yard."

"So you know why I'm here?"

"Yes, of course."

"How did you know about the cop?"

"I heard some cops in the hall talking and remembered seeing one go up to the roof earlier. So, when they were in the hall…"

"Start from the beginning, again, Mary. You saw a cop go up to the roof… what time?"

"I woke from my chair this afternoon and…"

"What time."

"I didn't look at the clock."

"Then, take a guess."

"It was before the boy downstairs went to the store for me."

"Okay, then, it had to be around three when the kid came home from school, right?"

"Yes, your right. Actually, it was before that, maybe 2:45-ish?"

"Go on."

"I heard someone come up the stairs. I went to the door to see who it was."

Mary hesitated in thought.

"And?"

"It was the cop. To tell you the truth, I was kind of glad…you know… with everything else that's been going on around here."

"Sure…did you get a good look at his face?"

"Yes, I've seen him before."

"Oh! Where?"

"On the street from my window, and also the same day the maintenance man was here."

"Valentine? The one who fixed the doors!"

"That's right."

"If I show you some pictures, do you think you could identify him?"

"The cop? Yes. I think so."

Williams took out six pictures of policemen in uniform and placed them on her lap.

Mary looked at each one carefully and stopped at the fifth one. "That's him! That's the one that was here both times."

"Both times? You're sure?"

"Yes! Once, when the maintenance guy was here and then again today, like I said."

"And you're absolutely positive about that?"

"I'm positive, and the other day, the maintenance guy read the name on his uniform out loud. It was Bob something."

"Bob Scanlon?"

"Yes! That's it…Bob Scanlon."

"Okay, that matches the name of the cop in the picture you just picked out. How about this last time, was there someone with him?"

"No, I didn't see anyone…only him."

"Not the maintenance man?"

"Definitely not! After the cop went up to the roof, I went back to my chair and fell asleep."

"Did you actually see him climb the ladder?"

"The cop? Yes…I did."

"By himself?"

"Oh, absolutely!"

"Did you hear anything after that?"

"No…like what?"

"Like anything!"

"No, I dozed off."

"Did you hear yelling or people talking up there?"

"No! When I woke up, the TV was still on, so I watched the news and some time later, I heard an ambulance outside and then some people in the hall right after that. Well…the police I mean. You know, in the hall. I was by the door."

"The Keyhole!"

"Yes. That's how I knew about the cop in the yard. I heard them talking."

"What about the kid?"

"What about him?"

"Did the kid go up to the roof?"

"I don't think so. I probably would have heard him if he had."

Williams toyed with his mustache while remaining focused on her. After a long pause, he finally said, "If you remember anything else about that kid or anything about what we talked about, give me a call.

8:32 P.M. The roof

"Where did Lieutenant Abrams go?" asked Captain Malone.

"The Deli to get something to eat," said O'Brien.

"He still has an appetite? Good for him. Did anybody talk to Scanlon's wife?"

"We're getting ready to drive over there, now," said Ted Williams.

The captain shined a flashlight on the capstone. "That was here all this time?"

"Yes, right there inside the chalk mark, Cap."

"Okay, what else ya got. Anyone see anything?"

O'Brien shook his head no, his lips pushing sideways into his cheek as he flipped through the pages from his notes. "No one downstairs saw or heard anything. Nope! I got nothing concrete, Cap."

"What about you, Williams, was it Scanlon, yesterday?"

"With the maintenance guy? That was Scanlon all right. We interviewed Valentine Castillo at his Hardware Store up the street on Nevins. He told me Scanlon had to write a report. A description of the rooms, he said."

"Bullshit! He had no business up here. The Barnes case was nearly closed at that time. Wasn't it?"

"Not totally."

"I'm not talking about City Hall and the 18th. I know all about that. I'm talking about right here!"

"Right, Cap! Yeah! We were done interviewing the building. Forensics was done, also."

"Okay, so apparently Scanlon was on the hunt for the money?"

"That's what we figured," said Don.

"Did we get any prints off the stone?"

"Nah, too porous. They got some off of the ladder though…and the hatch. The ones on the ladder were from Scanlon of course and some contamination from the cops that first answered the call. We also have both Joe Barnes and a kid from downstairs on the ladder as well as the metal hatch."

"What kid?"

"Uh…a kid named Diego Rivera. He lives in 1A with his mother."

"How big is this kid? What do we know about him?"

"I know what you're thinking, Cap, but he's only fourteen and about this short." Don held his opened hand out to indicate the correct height.

"When was he on the roof last? You interviewed him, didn't you?"

Don took out his note book and flipped to the page.

"Monday, April 24th, 240 Dean Street, apartment 1A. Spoke to…"

"Stop! Stop! I know it's Monday! I don't need all of that! I only want the time. When did you speak to him?"

"Almost two hours ago…6:43…in his apartment."

Good! And what did he say?"

Don continued to read from his notes.

Likes to watch pigeons on roof across yard
Looks for balls on roof

"Yeah, yeah, yeah! How about today…like this afternoon? Was the kid up here?"

"I was coming to that. I wanted to first verifying why we found his prints on the ladder."

Don looked for his place on the note pad.

Spent afternoon at friend Larry's house after school
Watched Westerns from 3:20 until 6:00

"Okay…so you checked that all out and the boy claims he wasn't up here today?"

"Yes, and that Larry kid's mother was home at the time. She backed up his story, and besides her, Mary, the lady in the front room, according to Ted here, saw Scanlon go up to the roof before 3:00…by himself."

"2:45," Detective Williams corrected.

Malone took off his captain's hat and ran gloved fingers through greying hair. He glanced at the pigeon coop, all settled in the glow of a street light, and then stepped to the edge. Below, the neighboring yard was softly illuminated by a night lamp from a kitchen window. In its expose lay the shepherd, curled tightly into a ball.

"Hey, so forget that. Are you guys thinkin' what I'm thinkin'?"

"He tripped on the capstone all by himself!" Williams said, matter of factly.

The captain nodded. "That's right! Scanlon was up here looking around, for what else…the money. He doesn't see the stone, or forgets that it's there, and over he goes."

"Then, how did the capstone get from the chimney to the back end of the roof?" Williams asked.

"Barnes! Who else! You said Scanlon came up here alone, right?"

"That's what Mary said, but that doesn't explain the capstone. Somebody else had to be up here at one time or another."

"The kid!" said Don.

Malone put his hands on his hips and stared into the distance. "Maybe! Did you ask him?"

"He doesn't remember seeing it there."

"When did you say the kid was here last?"

"I didn't!" Don checked his notes, turning and tracing the pages quietly with a moistened fingertip. "Okay…what I wrote down here was that it was a couple of weeks ago. The kid doesn't remember exactly when."

The captain, his hands now clasped behind his back, stared into the yard.

"He doesn't remember?…Humph!"

"You think we should bring him in and put a little pressure on him?" said Don.

"Pressure? What the hell for? Since he apparently wasn't up here today, we have nothing. Besides, with him being a minor and that alibi of his, we don't have enough just cause to do that. No, I get the feeling that this Barnes guy, or more than likely, his cohorts put that capstone there. It might have been loose already and they decided to threaten him with it."

"But Cap, Barnes was already dead when those guys showed up here. He was found in the park, remember?"

"I'm not talking about this time, O'Brien! They could have been here way before that and threatened him with the stone sometime back then. We really don't know how long that stone was laying there, now, do we?

"In the meantime, we don't have anything else to go on, and I don't see any reason to believe otherwise. Not only that, there's no blood on it, and according to the forensic report the only injuries on Scanlon were the ones he got from the fall."

"So, do you want us to give you the report the way it is?" said Don.

"Leave it on my desk. I'll stall headquarters for a few more days with some bullshit before we send it downtown. If nothing else turns up, we'll close the whole thing. For now, it looks like we're finished here. Whaddya say we get some coffee and donuts before you run over to the widow's house? They're two for one at Herzog's."

CHAPTER SEVEN
Loose ends and Loan Sharks

Diego turned the knob to his apartment door and opened it slowly. "Mom?"

"What took you so long? Are you okay? You don't look so good."

"I was hanging out with Larry."

"I told you to come right back with the money."

"I know Mom, but let me explain first."

"I was so worried! You didn't show him anything, did you?"

"Relax, Mom. No...I didn't!"

Exhausted, Diego locked the door. The steel box, he laid gently on the table.

To Ana, the plain steel container, tarnished and stained with soot, had a valueless quality to it. It was hard to imagine that within such an insignificant piece of tin lay nearly $10,000. She held onto the round, porcelain corner of the sink while staring at it.

"Mom..? I...I...never mind."

Diego couldn't hold the tragedy inside anymore. He wanted to tell her everything that had happened. If only he could say the words, but his emotions were getting in the way. He edged over to the sink and quietly put his arms around his mother, held her tightly and let a flood of uncontrolled tears spill out.

"Oh, God, Mom, I'm so sorry. I'm sorry, I'm sorry. I didn't mean it. It just happened."

The boy's cries became louder. All he wanted right now was to hold onto her, the only person in the whole world who had the power to make everything better. He said nothing else. For the moment, he could forget about all that had just happened. What really mattered was that he was inside his mother's arms where he could once again be her little boy. The soft touch of her fingers running through his dark curls relaxed him. He stayed there, whimpering with his face to her warm breast.

"Diego...this will all pass with time. There is nothing that cannot be fixed. Come sit here on the couch with me. Let's see what is inside that box."

Her head lifted and she leaned it back, smiled at his upturned face and wiped his cheeks. "Are you okay?"

(*Sniff!*) "It's...it's...not the money that's bothering me."

"If it's not the money, then tell me what it is?"

"Not now, please? I promise I'll tell you. Let me calm down first, please?"

"Take all the time you need, Diego," She continued to run her fingers through his hair.

Sitting next to her on the couch with the box in his lap, Diego left it closed and toyed with the metal latch. "You know something?"

Her brows raised.

"I haven't cried in years. I feel so stupid."

"Why do you feel stupid? You should not feel that way. The strongest man can cry, even the president."

"You think so?"

"I know so."

Her son let out a slight laugh.

"Even Bruno de San Martino," she said.

"The wrestler? No...I don't think so, Mom."

"Well, I do. If he has something to cry about, he's going to cry, too."

Diego felt along the edges of the steel box.

"Are you going to open it?" she asked.

Silent, he thought about the cop and the awful fall. It kept replaying inside his mind and wouldn't go away. He forced himself to think of better times, like his first look down the chimney and the elation he had felt, the money and how he spent it in his thoughts.

Ana tilted her head and looked sideways at him. "Well?"

"You want to see it?"

"That's up to you."

She clasped her hands together, relaxed her raised shoulders and took a deep breath. She watched as he flipped the catch to the clasp, unhooked it and then finally raised the lid. The top-most corner of the loosely bound wrapping started to unfold all by itself, though barely. However, it was enough to see a hint of the forest green color underneath. Her lips parted. She could see the number ten in the corner and then the rest of the stack as her son removed the rest of the brown wrapping.

"Open your hands, Mom."

Ana complied, outstretching her arms and spreading trembling fingers into mid-air. She put the palms together side by side and was surprised by the weight of the money when her son dropped it into her hands. She immediately placed the bills on her lap and proceeded to thumb through them.

"You must not spend a penny of this money."

"Why?"

"It belongs to bad people."

"You mean the ones that were in Mary's room?"

"Yes!"

Thinking for a while, she finally said, "Let's find a good place to hide it until we know what to do."

"Mom, about that thing I was going to tell you before. Do you remember all the cop cars that were outside a few hours ago?"

"What about them?"

"That was because of me."

The most surprised look Diego had ever seen on his mother's face, glared back at him.

He continued. "I thought Karen would have told you by now, but she's probably so scared with everything that's been happening in this building that she's afraid to leave her apartment.

"When I was on the roof this afternoon to get this money, a cop was up there. I don't know how, but he must have figured everything out. He threatened me and punched me in the stomach. It hurt so bad, I thought I was going to throw up. I tried to tell him I didn't know anything, but he found the money anyway. It was in the chimney where I hid it. That's where I found it in the first place."

"Inside the chimney?"

"Yes, that's where I left it, because I didn't know where else to hide it. It seemed like a pretty good hiding place at the time."

"How did he know where it was?"

"He saw me looking at the chimney. He got real mad and tripped, so I ducked down. I didn't want to get hit again mom, and…and…"

A stream of tears returned. Diego laid his head on his mother's lap, shaking and bawling like a two year old child.

"He tripped, and…and…he…fell. He fell off the roof. Oh, Mom…it's all my fault."

Both shocked and frightened by what she just heard, Ana leaned over Diego's quivering body, embraced him and continued to run shaking fingers through his hair. Finally, in slow, softly uttered words, she said, "If he tripped, then it's not your fault."

His head in her lap, he cried, "But…but Mom, if I didn't go up there just then, he wouldn't have fallen."

"Did you think that he may have wanted to push you off the roof to keep the money?"

"No, I didn't think of that!"

"Right now we don't know this. Only God knows. God knows who the bad people are, so, maybe he found this one.

"Don't believe this was all your fault when it was the policeman who did this to himself. Why don't you blame me? I was the one who told you to go up there in the first place.

Outside, leaning over the edge of the stoop, Butchie backed away from Ana's window. The boy had been out there watching the building for the last two hours like his father had ordered him to do every evening that week.

Surprised, nonetheless, by what he just witnessed, Butchie now knew that both the mob and his father had been right all along. The money was still in the house and he needed to tell them. Immediately!

One hour later

The steel box still lay on the table. Ana looked around the large room, yet again, for a good place to hide the money. "What about under the sink?"

"No…what if one day we need a plumber and we forget it's there."

"Yes, you're right. Inside the TV, maybe?"

"Same thing, Mom. We could get robbed when we're out and the money would be carried away with the TV."

"So, what do you think?"

"I think we should think really hard. Something will come up, eventually."

(Silence)

After a while longer, they took a quick look at one another, shook heads and resumed their focus on the box.

Five minutes later.

"Think of anything?"

Ana's hands folded in front of her face with the forefingers pointing like a tent over her lips. She sullenly shook her head no.

(KNOCK! KNOCK! KNOCK!)

"Shh!" Ana covered her son's mouth.

(KNOCK! KNOCK! KNOCK!)

Both remained quiet and stared at the door.

"It's me, Bill. Anybody home?"

"Just a minute!" Diego blurted out.

Ana glared at him as if he had gassed the room with one of his notorious farts. With both fist, she punched the cushions of the sofa and raised her finger to her lips. **"Shhh!"**

"I need to talk to ya'll, Diego, it's important."

"Just a minute, Bill."

"Diego! No!" Ana loudly whispered, her entire body falling limp while looking crushed and defeated. "Why did you do that!"

"I'll be right there! Diego said."

"The drawer! Put it inside the drawer for now!" said Ana.

"Yes, suh!" Bill loudly said. "Ah knows it's gittin' late, but ah needs to talk to yo' momma."

"Hang on, Bill!" Snatching the box from the table, Diego opened the bottom of three drawers and pushed the clothes to the side. He placed the box in the middle and covered it with socks, closed the drawer and looked over his shoulder for her approval.

"Ain't no rush. Go ahead and finish up with whatever it was ya'll was doin' in there. But tomorra? Tomorra we is a gonna take care of a snake."

Diego cocked his head and looked questioningly at his mother.

Just as confused, Ana crossed her eyes, shrugged her shoulders and returned a funny face. Like Diego, she had no idea what Bill Jackson was talking about.

"Come in, Mr. D," said Diego, as he opened the door. "What were you saying about a snake?"

"Ratzstein! That old snake in the grass! Why, that man...hello, Missus Ana."

"Ratzfarb? The principal?" Diego asked.

"Yes, suh! Ratzfarb, Ratzstein, whatever that man's name is. The time to kill a snake is when he raises his head, and by golly if he don't raise that fat head o' his, I'm gonna drag it on outta his smelly hole with the rest of his sorry ass along with it."

"But…what about him?"

"I don't sees how that man coulda made it to where he is today. Ya'll cayn't git no lower than a snake in a wagon rut, and by God, that man sho must know the taste o' dirt.

"Ma apology, Missus Ana, but that man done got me all riled up."

Diego continued to look puzzled. "Why be so mad? I thought that whole thing about the darts was over and done with?"

"Ah thought so, too. But you know what? Ah been had alla dis here cookin' inside ma brain like white lightenin' in a slow still. And ya'll know what ah figa'd? There ain't no way ya'll shouda carried that blame all by yo'self, when we all knows you ain't the one that done did it."

"Bill, take it easy. There's not much we can do, anymore. It's too late to change any of that?"

"What if ah was to tell you that I wanted to meet that boy who throwed them darts and have a little southern style chat with him. How would you feel about that?"

"As far as I'm concerned, I already let it go."

"No, suh! That ain't the proper way to be a man. What all is that boy's name, anyhow?"

"The one that brought the darts to school? Willy Goodwin!"

"Colored boy?"

"How did you know?"

"Ain't no white boy 'round these parts with a name like Willy!"

"What are you going to say to him? You know he's not going to admit anything."

"Not right off the bat, he ain't. Oh, heck, I surely knows that, too. But down where I's comes from, we got our ways. You cayn't git away with much down there. Ever'body knows ever'body and sooner or later, the truth is goin' to come out."

"Not here, unless you're a boy scout or an altar boy."

"We'll see about that. Just point his silly ass out to me tomorra after school and I'll do the rest. But don't be standin' there. I'll introduce my own self."

"All right, Bill, if you think so."

"Son, ah know I'm right!"

Five minutes after midnight
One block away on Dean Street

"How long have we been parked out here," said the Geek.

"It's gotta be at least two hours," said Butchie's father, John Kelly, a.k.a., Jersey Johnny, leaning against the front passenger door with his foot resting on the dash."

Sprawled out across the back seat, Fast Eddie asked, "Are dey gonna post dat cop in front of Joe's building all night?"

"How should we know, knucklehead," said the Geek. "Just sit back there and stop asking so many questions. You're starting to get on my nerves like Tommy did."

"Yeah, yeah!"

"Dis is a fuckin' waste o' my time," said Jersey Johnny."

The Geek smirked. "You're right, mine, too. That cop ain't leaving. With everything that's been going on in that building, the place is hot, that's why. By the way, thanks for the call, we appreciate that."

"Don't mention it. One hand washes de udder one, right?"

The Geek shook Jersey Johnny's extended hand. "Yeah, thanks. How are your boys doing here in Brooklyn?"

"Priddy good! We're trying to get control o' da udda side of Smith Street, but the Italians won't budge. They're all over Carol Gardens and Cobble Hill."

"Don't push too hard, any war you get into is going to affect us in the Kitchen and I'm sure you know that."

"Yeah, we know. Right now, we'll settle for da few crumbs we can get, we're not greedy. Besides, we got everything around the bridges sewed up, includin' all of Fulton Street."

Hey, how sure are you that that kid of yours saw the money in the front room?"

"My kid ain't stupid! If he says he saw da money, den he did."

"What didja give him for hangin' around here for the last few days." (*Snap*) "A coupla bucks?" said Fast Eddie.

Jersey Johnny twisted around and stared at him lying across the seat with his head propped up on the arm rest. "So, what business is dat of yours **what** I give him?"

"Just askin', dat's all!" (Snap...Pop)

"I knew that money was in the building somewhere." said the Geek. "Where does your kid know him from? They friends, or something?"

"Maybe dey go to da same school," said Fast Eddie.

"Who was askin' you? Didn't I just tell you to shut up?"

"Mumble, mumble." (Snap...Chew...Chew)

"He knows da kid from stick ball. They're on different teams," said Jersey Johnny.

"I'm done with this crap. Let's go!" said the Geek. We're gonna drop you off at the house and move on. We got other business to attend to tonight. It's not like this is the only money we gotta collect out here."

Johnny took his foot off the dash. "Pass by the house real slow, foist, I wanna see if a cop is in dat squad car or if it's empty."

The Geek cranked the engine and pulled out of the parking space. He rolled to the stop sign on Bond Street, making sure to make a full stop as opposed to a rolling one.

"Stay down when we get to the house, Eddie, I don't want the cop to see any more guys in here other than us two in the front seat."

"I see him. He's got his head layin' back. He's probably sleeping," said Jersey Johnny.

"The hell with it. We'll come back tomorrow."

3:05 P.M. Outside P.S.6

"That's him right there! That's Willy Goodwin!" Said Diego.

"Good! Now git yo'salf on out o' here. I'll talk to ya'll lata," said Bill.

"Lots of luck!"

"Don't worry 'bout nuthin', ya hear?"

"Let me know how you..."

"I know...I know. Go on with you, now. Ah don't want that boy to see us togetha."

With a heavy backpack pulling down on his shoulders, Willy Goodwin passed through the school gates. He headed toward the Gowanus Housing Projects on Baltic Street which was only a few blocks away. Forced to stop at the light for passing cars on the corner of Hoyt Street, he leaned on a lamp post while waiting for the traffic to clear the intersection.

Bill sidled his tall frame to within inches of the kid. He sensed that the boy was looking up, but didn't readily acknowledge him. Just before the light turned green, he faced him fully. "Willy Goodwin?"

Taken aback, the boy appeared surprised. "How did you know my name?"

"Oh, wale, because you is an important man around here, that's all."

"I am?"

"Yes, suh! A vera important man!"

"How do you mean?"

"Wale, because you, Mista Goodwin, is the solution to the whole case."

"Me? What case?"

"The case of the poorly learned versus an innocent man accused of somethin' he ain't neva did."

"I don't think I'm following you."

"Oh...you will! Let me explain it to ya'll, Willy. Fust of all, I'd like to shake your hand and introduce masalf...if I may! Mista William Calhoun Jackson the Fust, and I am maghty proud to say hello to such a fine gentleman like yo'self on this fine sunny, January day."

Willy didn't know what to make of it all, but by now, curiosity had gotten the best of him. Besides, with them being this close to the school grounds, he couldn't be sure whether or not the old man was somehow connected to it.

"Is you a God fearin' man, Mista Goodwin?"

"I go to church on Sunday."

"Now, that there ain't exactly what ah meant. What ah is talkin' 'bout, is what be inside that little ticker of yaws?"

"I believe in God, sir."

"All right, then, we is halfway there, son! So, is it safe to say that you, Mista Goodwin, believe yo'self to be that honest and righteous man I'm talkin' 'bout?"

With a quick nod of the head, Willy confirmed it. "Yes, I do."

"All right, then. Now, that leads me to the next question. Is you ready?"

"Yes, sir, I'm...I'm ready!"

"If someone, let's say a good friend or even a relative was to do you wrong, like take your bicycle, or maybe even that bag your carrying and sell it somewhere, would that make you mad?"

"It sure would."

"Good! And if that same fella went and did something real bad like and then tells the po-leece that it was Willy Goodwin who done did it, how would that make you feel?"

"Whoa! Not very good. Hell, I'd kick his ass in."

"As much as you maght thank it be a good idea to do that, Willy, we don't always git that opportunity. Sometimes, all those involved might get rounded up into a room and there wouldn't be nothin' left that little ol' Willy Goodwin could do but sit there a shakin' and trying to tell ever'body that it wasn't him."

"Hey, that isn't fair! If I didn't do it, I shouldn't be punished for it, either."

Bill raised his opened hands toward the sky. "Well, glory be on high, Almighty. Now, let me shake yo' hand, Mr. Goodwin. You done restored ma faith in humanity."

"I did?"

"Would you mind if we cross this here street and set on that bench. I won't take much more of your time, I promise. So, Willy, how does it feel to know yourself a little betta and that you are indeed a righteous and honorable young man?"

"I guess it feels good. I sure wouldn't want nobody to disrespect me like that."

"Now, **that! That** is what I is waitin' to hear. You said it all in a nutshell. You said the magic word before it even got a chance to pass through my own, sad, raggedy, ol' lips. **Respect!** That is the gist of the whole matta right there. **Respect!** And right now, I have the deepest respect for you, Mista Willy E. Goodwin."

"You even know my middle initial?"

"It's scribbled right there on your bag, son. Anyways, from one respectful and honorable person to another of equal character and upstandin' for-t-tude an' proper count-t-nances, I want to ask you to do me one fava."

"Sure, like what?"

"I want you to right a wrong that I know you done did. And here's the thang. Ain't nothin' more cleansin' to the soul than rightin' a wrong. Do you believe that?"

"I do...honest!"

"Oh, ah knows you do. Ah can tell. Are you ready to cleanse that soul and start fresh?"

"Yes, sir! ...I think."

"Then I need you to make amends with a boy in your class concerning a little thing about throwing darts at a teacher. Diego Rivera, he's in your class, ain't he?"

"How do you know all this?"

"Ah have my ways. And now that we both understand one another, what do you say we go and pays Mr. Rat-stein a little visit?"

"Mr. Ratzfarb? The principal? Geez…I don't know about that. I'll be in an awful lot of trouble if I did."

"You mean like Diego was?"

"I'm really sorry that ever happened. I like Diego. I hated that he got blamed for throwing the darts, I really did. It's just that I couldn't bring myself to say it was me."

"Took the easy way out, didn't you?"

"I guess so."

"And that's okay. We all make mistakes in life. The smart peoples be the ones that learn from them. And you is one of the smartest boys ah know."

"Me?"

"Yes, you is! It's jest that you be seein' the light anew, now ain't that so?"

"I…I…I guess so!"

"You ain't goin' to be afraid to talk to no principal, is you? Cause if that man even starts to pucker up them chubby lips o' his to say the wrong thang to you, I'll be the fust one to **smack** him up side his head."

"Ha ha! You will?"

"Hell, son! Ain't nobody goin' to mess with a fellow upstandin' man like you and get away with it with me. Not if ah can help it. I'll be standin' right behind you, Mista Willy E. Goodwin."

"If you really think I should…I guess…well, I guess…I could do it."

"Willy, I am so proud o' ya'll. I'd share a fox hole with you any day."

"You mean, like, to fight the Germans together?"

"Son, that wars been over nearly two decades, already. The Communist or whoever, it don't matta who the enemy be. The enemy, that's all."

Bill's arms waved around animatedly as he continued. "We could load our machine gun and point that old Betsy up the hill and drop thems suckas down like wooden ducks in an arcade game."

"Do I get to shoot?"

"Sho can! While you is a pullin' on that trigga, I'll be feedin' ol' betsy a belt load of ammunition. Now how's that sound?"

"Slap me five, Mr. Jackson. I like that part."

"Hey, guess what? Hows 'bout you and me, bypassing' that ol' fool Ratzstein, and go on straight to the top?"

"The top? The top of what?"

4:10 P.M.
Assemblyman James Richards Office
Schermerhorn Street.

The thick, plate glass doors to Mr. Richards' office building were huge. Willy chose the brass revolving doors instead, just so he could push his way inside. Along with Bill, they looked for the assemblyman's office among the tenant list inside a glass enclosed cabinet.

"There's his name right there, Assemblyman James Richards, room four-hundred and nine," said Willy, pleased at having found it so readily.

Bill had already seen it when they first looked. "Yup, Assemblyman James Richards, E. S. Q., 52nd District. That man is a lawya. I didn't even know that. Good Work, son. Let's go on up."

"Can I hit the button?"

"Sure can. Numba fo'."

Bill exited the elevator ahead of Willy and followed the numbers on the office doors upwards from 400. As they crossed the off white tile, their winter boots resounded loudly through the labyrinths of long, empty hallways.

"I'm scared," said Willy.

Looking down at the boy, Bill fondly put a hand on his shoulder and sternly said, "Now, why did you and I set up all night in that foxhole gettin' alla that ammo ready for a good fight? You ain't gonna jump out of that hole and run the other way, is you?"

"Heck, no, Mr. Jackson!"

"Sergeant, to you Corporal!"

"Oh yeah! I meant to say Sergeant Bill."

"It ain't like you gotta skip town 'cause yo' girlfrien' Opal got pregnant."

"Who's Opal?"

"Neva mind, son. Did you clean ol' Betsy with oil, like ah told you, Corporal?"

"The machine gun? Yes, sir, Sarge! It's ready and pointed at the hill."

"Now, you gettin' it. You in the right frame of mind." Bill patted him on the shoulder. "Here we is…room four o nine. Prepare yo'salf, soldier, we is a goin' in!"

Bill's tall frame shadowed the opaque glass as he held open the office door for Willy.

"May I help you?" said a thin, plain Jane of fifty plus, her bouffant style flipped upward at the ends and dyed dark brown.

"We is here to see Mista Richards."

"He's busy right now and he has a meeting to go to in fifteen minutes."

"That so? Could ya'll maybe tell him Bill Jackson is in to see him, ma'am?"

The lady, now standing behind her desk, put the black receiver to a rotary phone down and removed a pair of dark rimmed glasses. "He's busy! Perhaps you could come back tomorrow! And I also suggest you call first."

"Yes, ma'am. But this sho' is important."

"I already told you, mister, he's very busy."

"Now, ma'am…ain't no need to get sharp, all ah is trying to…"

James Richard's door opened. "Bill! I knew that was your voice I heard… come on in."

The secretary glared back. "But, the meeting, Mr. Richards. You have a meeting in fifteen minutes."

"That can wait. Give them a call for me. Come on in Bill. Good to see you."

Bill stepped lively into the oversized office where the loud sound of his boots became muffled as he crossed a circular, Oriental rug.

The assemblyman-lawyer took his seat behind a wide and very heavy mahogany desk, picked out a cigar from a half filled box and settled into a leather recliner. He gave the cigar a prolonged whiff, licked the length of it and leaned the chair way back with his legs crossed to light it up.

"I need a break. I've been running around all day with these confounded meetings. Enough is enough. Have a cigar, Mr. Jackson, and how's Diego, by the way?"

"He's fine, doin' real well, he is. Actually, he be the verra reason why me and Willy here is where we is, right now, suh."

"Hey, let's enjoy the moment. Did you want that cigar?"

"No, I don't smoke, but thank you kindly, anyways."

"That's surprising. Isn't the South the cigarette capitol of the world?"

"We is gots lots o' tobacca farms, that's fo' sho'."

"Aren't you going to take a seat?"

Bill looked around himself. Behind, were four, deep-brown, top grain, split leather, tri-tone, hand rubbed recliners. So as not to look unaccustomed to such opulence, he sat unhesitatingly and crossed his legs.

Willy did the same. The boy checked around for a way to recline the chair and found the oak handle sticking up from the side. As the other two talked, he played around with it to try to make the chair work.

"So what brings you to my office, Bill?"

His arm outstretched, Bill gestured toward the boy, and in his best effort toward well-spoken, colloquial speech, said, "Wale, I have here, seated on my left, a proud memba' of the Honorable and Righteous Societa, of which we have two memba's…hims and me."

Amused, Mr. Richards kept a serious demeanor; for the boys sake.

Willy finally got the chair to work. His entire body suddenly and forcefully jolted backwards.

"Continue, Mr. Jackson, I sense something very important brewing here. Please, go on."

"Wale, it's thisa way. Here at ma side is a Mr. Willy E. Goodwin, who in a moment of poor judgement, threw three darts at…"

Bill went on to explain the entire dart incident to the assemblyman and how Diego had gotten blamed for it.

"And therefore, as sole owner and executor of the three darts to which he no longer has possession…"

"And who, pray tell, is the new possessor of the aforementioned darts?" Mr. Richards interrupted.

"A one, Mr. Ratzstein, suh. Principal in residence at P.S, 6."

"He lives there?"

"Well, no…uh…uh, I's only added that in for a little dignitary flavor, if you get the gist of what ah mean?"

"Okay, I get it. So, Mr. Goodwin, you're the one that actually threw the darts?"

"Yes, Mr. Richards and I'm really sorry about that."

"Hey, I'm sure if you could take it all back, you would, wouldn't you, Mr. Goodwin?"

"In a heartbeat. Yes, sir!"

The door opened.

"Your meeting, Mr. Richards, it's getting late!"

"Yes, I know! Cancel it!"

"But, they're in 211 waiting for you."

"That's all right. Tell them all to go home and I'll work out another arrangement with them. Heck, it's almost dinner time, anyway. Don't these people have families?"

"Sir, I don't think you..."

"That's all, Miss Dugan. In fact you should be going home as well."

The door closed.

"Some people take things too much to heart. Now, where were we? The darts! I'm glad you came forward with this, Goodwin. It takes a stand up man to do that. I like your honesty."

Willy folded his hands, expecting the worse.

"All that's left, now, is to give the principal a call, but I'll have to do that tomorrow."

"Willy is a good boy, Mista Richards. Ah can vouch for him, masalf."

"That's good enough for me, Bill. In the meantime, Mr. Goodwin, I'll need a promise from you."

"Sir?"

"Let's put it this way. We'll make a gentlemen's agreement between you and me. If you show a steady improvement between now and your last report card for the year, and I want that last one to have nothing less than a b, I'll find you a spot in our summer camp program."

"You will?"

"Yes, and that's a promise."

"Where?"

"This year, the kids are going to the Adirondacks."

"Wow! That's great! Where's that?"

"The mountains!"

"The mountains?"

"That's right, and do you know what they do there?"

"Swim?"

"Swim, and that's not all. They have archery and baseball and basketball..."

"I can shoot a bow?"

"Absolutely! You can camp, go canoeing, hike through the mountains and make a campfire at night. There's all kinds of fun things to do. So, do you want to go?"

"Can I really?"

"Of course you can. Just bring me those a's and b's."

"I will, Mr. Richards."

"Bring your next report card right here to my office and we'll go over it together."

The following morning
P.S. 6 Principal's Office

(*Phone ringing*)

"Principal Ratzfarb, how can I assist you?"

"It's James Richards, how's everything going, John?"

"Well, well! I haven't heard from you since the summer when we played golf on Staten Island."

"How's your putting arm?"

"Getting better. I have a green runner in my office that I practice on."

"Good… good."

"What can I do for you?"

"It's nothing major, just a small favor."

"Sure, anything?"

"Do you remember a boy named Diego Rivera?"

"Yes, smart kid. I'm skipping him a grade. Why do you ask?"

"I'm concerned about an incident involving darts sometime last month."

"Yes, that was him, but we took care of that and straightened the kid out and now he's a good student."

"I see! I'm sorry, John, but that's not how I'm seeing it."

"What do you mean? What exactly are you talking about?"

"I had the kid who threw those darts in my office yesterday. He came in with Bill Jackson. Bill says he knows you?"

"Jackson…Jackson…hm. Yes, that's the man who came by with Rivera. His mother couldn't come. He's a neighbor, supposedly."

"Yes…well, he does some work around the house from time to time, that's why I know him, and Diego, also."

"So, now you want me to exonerate him because he does work for you?"

"No! I want you to exonerate him because Willy Goodwin admitted to me in my office that it was him all along. The darts were his."

"Damn! Why can't we leave this alone? What's the big deal?"

"Diego's a good kid with a future. He's already proved himself with good grades. Why do you want to brand him with horse shit like this on his record, when I just gave you the name of the kid who claimed responsibility?"

"Because, I have better things to do with my time. Hello…hello…hello… James? Are you still there?"

"Yes, I'm still here. Look, John, I don't want to go over your head, but if I have to I will."

"For this lousy crap? Don't you have better things to do with your time?"

"This **is** that 'better thing', John. It's not only important to Diego, it's important to me. What are you planning to do about this, because if we can't resolve it over the phone, I'll be forced to make a call to your district superintendent?"

"You don't have to do that. I'll take care of it. I'll see that Goodwin kid in my office first thing tomorrow."

"And lay off him, he didn't have to come forward. The worst thing you could do right now would be to break his trust by punishing him. Make him write an essay or something easy. There's no need to go any further than that."

"Yeah, all right James. I'll take care of it."

"I got your word on it, right, John?"

"Of, course! I said I'd take care of it."

That afternoon
Diego's apartment

"Come in, Mister Richards."

"Hi, Ana. Diego around?"

"He went to the store for Maria. He'll be back soon. Coffee?"

"No thanks. Mind if I sit?"

"Oh, I'm sorry! Please…have a seat."

It was hard for Richards to focus on conversation while looking around the room. The plastic curtains and dated, cheaply crafted furniture, pulled at his heartstrings. 'Though neat with everything in its place, even the lone, frameless picture of a tropical beach scene hanging on the wall, spoke of paucity and the few basic essentials present.

"I need to see Mr. Jackson, but I...don't know where he lives."

"He lives someplace on Bergen Street. Diego can show you."

"You won't mind if I wait?"

"No, that's okay. No coffee?"

"I'm fine, Ana, thank you?"

***

The drab hall to the Jackson's rear room smelled stale and musty. It took Richards a few seconds to accustom himself to the dim light of the hallway's 25 watt bulb. The narrow walls had been painted a dull gray sometime back during the Cretaceous Era with no thought as to a contrasting trim color.

"Is that their door?"

"Yes, that's it," said Diego.

"Mr. Jackson!"

"Glory be! That you, Mista Richards?" said, Bill, from the other side of the door.

The door opened.

"Well come on in. Good to see ya'll...and there be Diego, too?"

James Richards stepped inside and was taken aback by what he saw. Though clean, the sad condition and day to day existence in a room that was not only a living room, but a bedroom and kitchen all wrapped in one, was appalling and far worse than what he had seen at Diego's.

Embarrased for not only himself, but for Beulah as well, Bill remained proud and spoke with energetic enthusiasm. "Miss Beulah, this here be the assemblyman I been talkin' 'bout. This is ma wife, Beulah, Mista Richards."

"Please to meet you, Mrs. Jackson."

"Oh, shesh! Just Beulah, that's all." She waved at Diego. "Git on over here and give Momma Beulah some sugar."

Following a tight hug, she wiped her worn hands on an apron and shook Mr. Richard's.

Bill said, "What all brings two fine, decent folk like ya'll to visit our humble abode?"

Mr. Richards said, "The reason for our visit is because I have some good news. Mr. Ratzfarb agreed to clear Diego of all wrong doing concerning the dart incident."

"Glory be! That sho is good to hear."

"You get most of the credit, Mr. Jackson and I know Diego especially appreciates what you did for him."

"We got to celebrate," said Beulah. Want some corn braid?"

"Actually, I'm heading home for dinner, but I hear your corn bread has quite a reputation."

"Let me send you on home with some."

"That's kind of you, Beulah. I'll have it with my evening coffee."

The following day
Gowanus Housing project
211 Hoyt Street

Property Managers office
(Phone ringing)
Clerk, "Hello?"

"Hello, this is Assemblyman James Richards from the 52nd District, Downtown. I'd like to know the procedure for applying for an apartment there. I'm speaking in behalf of a gentleman acquaintance of mine."

"Yes, no problem, Mr. Richards. He'll have to fill out an application. It will go under review and if everything is in order and he qualifies, he'll go on a list."

"How long is the list?"

"Is this for a one bedroom or a two bedroom?"

"A one bedroom."

"For a one bedroom, the waiting list runs for four years, and presently, where up to number...hold on Mr. Richards while I get that information for you. This will only take a minute. Do you want me to call you back?"

"No, I'll wait, thank you."

(A few minute later)

"Hello? Are you still there, Mr. Richards?"

"Yes, I'm still here."

(Papers rustling)

"Presently, we're up to number 28 on a list of…of…"

(More papers rustling)

"557 applicants."

"That's crazy. Why so many?"

"This is a nice project we have here. It's quite desirable. We're near Downtown and the subway line is only a few blocks away, so the commute to Manhattan is a short ride of only a few stations. Besides that, the cost for our city apartments are far below that of market value, but I'm sure you are already aware of that, Mr. Richards."

"Yes, that's the reason for the call. Isn't there some way that you and I could perhaps circumnavigate that little time consuming inconvenience?"

"None that I know of, rules being what they are, that is."

(A long pause)

"Mr. Richards?"

"Oh, yes, I'm sorry. I was just thinking. So there's no other way to do this?"

"Not through me. Would you like to talk to the project manager? I can switch you there now, If you like?"

"Yes, and thanks for your help."

(RING…RING)

"Project manager, Whelans speaking."

"Good Morning. This is Assemblyman James Richards from the 52nd District, Downtown. I have an acquaintance and his wife who are in dire need of immediate housing. I know there are procedures at hand, but if there is any…"

"I'm sorry to have to interrupt you, Mr. Richards, but we do have a waiting list."

"Yes, I'm aware of that, but the next list is probably, what, a few years down the road?"

"That's right, and there's no way I can tell you where on that new list your acquaintance will be placed. The wait could go for as long as another four to eight years from now."

"Four to eight years? I don't know if they have that much time left on this earth. These are elderly people, Mr. Whelans."

"Believe me, there are a lot of sad stories out there, and I've heard them all."

"I'm sure you have. But you see, Mr. Whelans, we have a real health issue here. The place they live in is crawling with vermin."

"Like a lot of other apartments in the city, Mr. Richards."

"Yes, but allow me to finish, please. These are elderly people. They live in one room. The bed is in the same place as the kitchen. The bathroom's in the hall…"

"Like a lot of other people out there."

"All right…all right, that may be true, but could you imagine your own mother living out her last years in squalor?"

"Hey, look! My mother prepared herself for old age. She married well and invested well. That's why she and my father have what they…"

"Wait! Hold on! That's not the same thing! These are poor, colored folks from the Deep South. What opportunities do you think they had growing up in the early 1900's, with no education and having to go out in the work force at an age when you were probably riding your little bicycle with training wheels and looking forward to summers off from school, not having to break your back…"

"Okay…okay, you're absolutely right. I agree. I didn't mean to upset you. I apologize. Sometimes I forget about the horrific lives some of these people have had. Let's face it. It's all around us, but we can't help everybody."

"So, what are you saying? Can you help them, or not?"

"Not with the present structure we have. Look, I really would like to help you, especially with you being a public official, but I just don't know if…"

"So, that's it, there's nothing you can do?"

"Oh…uh…I'm not exactly saying that…no. How about, I say what I'm about to say in a different way?"

"What do you mean?"

"Suppose you and I start a new conversation that has nothing to do with what we just talked about, and maybe we could go from there."

"I'm not sure I'm following you, but go ahead, I'm listening."

"Yes…good! Mr. Richards, I've been having the hardest time with the zoning Department. For years, I've been back and forth with them trying to get a permit so I can have a third bathroom installed in my limestone."

"Where's the location?"

"Park Slope?"

"Park Slope? Where in Park Slope is it?"

"Twelfth Street and Prospect Park West."

"That's right at the edge of my district. I live on Union Street between fifth and sixth. We're neighbors!"

"Well I'll be darned? So, Mr. Richards…is there any way you can help me with that?"

"The permit! Of course! That won't be a problem. Give me your address and I'll get on the phone right now. I'll get you a permit. As long as you have the square footage, I don't see why they're giving you such a hard time."

"It's the Landmarks Preservation Commission and their historical bullshit that's throwing a monkey wrench into this whole thing."

"I didn't get your first name, by the way?"

"Tom!"

"Tom, I'm James. I don't know why they're giving you such a hard time. As far as I know, they only have a say as to the outside of the structure. I don't see why they're troubling you with this. Let me make that call and I'll get back to you as soon as I get word."

An hour and a half later

"Project Manager, Whelans speaking."

"Yes, hello, it's James Richards."

"James, I've been waiting for your call with baited breath."

"Good news! It's in the mail! I never did get your address, so I took the liberty of having them mail it to your office."

"Great! That's fine, thank you. My wife will be so pleased to hear that."

"Good! Say, since we're neighbors, Tom, why don't you and your wife stop by for cocktails this evening. I'll get the fireplace going and we can play Scrabble. Do you play?"

"My wife does. Yes, sure, we're not doing anything."

"So…uh…what's going to happen now with my two acquaintances?"

"Don't worry, James. I already have that all figured out. You can see the place tonight. It's just been renovated and painted and it's on the second floor of an elevated building. My head clerk caught it just in time. Another day and it would have been assigned to someone on the list."

Gowanus Housing Project
Building 8 APT 2B

That evening

"Are you ready, Beulah?" asked James Richards.

"Ready as I'll ever be, ah reckon."

A young girl from the office handed her the key.

Beulah nervously inserted it into the key hole with *trembling fingers. She twisted the door knob and* opened the door to the smell of fresh paint. Beulah, Bill, Assemblyman Richards, Diego and the clerk from the office, all stepped inside. Large, west facing casement windows defined the living room with an expansive view of a tree-lined walkway one story below. Newly laid schoolroom tiles graced the floor.

Beulah started to cry.

"Now, don't be cryin' like a fat girl sittin' home on prom night. That's only goin' to start yo' Daddy in on it, and I ain't about to shame masalf in front of Mr. Richards." Bill grabbed her hand and walked her into the kitchen.

"It's yeller, Poppa. I always wanted a yeller kitchen. An' will you look at that? Glory be!" She opened the door to the refrigerator. "Look how big this ice box is, Poppa? You see the size of this here?"

Bill said, "We ain't neva lived in a place like this. I don't know what to say that'd be fittin', Mr. Richards?"

"I have all the appreciation I need just watching the two of you. Come take a look at this, your own bathroom. It's that door right there. By the way, your monthly obligation will be far less than what you were paying for that one room on Bergen Street."

Beulah rubbed her eyes. "Oh, Lord have mercy, Mr. Richards. And for a palace like this here with our vera own private bathroom?"

Diego held the door open for her. Beulah looked inside and marveled at the glistening subway tiles and unblemished fixtures.

"There ain't a chip on nary a thang in here."

"Not one chip," Bill added. "My word, if it don't look all brand spankin' new."

"Hey Poppa?"

"Yes, Missus Jackson?"

"You know how we get up in the middle of the night sometimes, and we be going all a the way down the hall for the bathroom when that floor be so cold you be thankin' you is steppin' on snow and ice. You can't see nothin' cause the light is so low, and us all groggy eyed 'cuz we just woke up. The cocka roaches be crunchin' under yo' bare feet and Lord knows what else?"

The stern faced girl from the office, quickly responded. "Not here, ma'am. We don't tolerate pest. If you ever see one, make sure you call maintenance right away."

Beulah shook her hand. "We ain't a gonna carry narry a one to this pretty place. I can promise you that."

"There's a bedroom right over there," said Diego.

Looking perplexed, Beulah asked, "You mean this ain't all of it, Diega?"

"This is a lot nicer than our place," he said.

"Give me a little time. I'll work on that…" said the assemblyman, "…and you can tell Ana what I said."

"Hey, Poppa?"

"Yes, Missus Jackson!"

"Does ya'll 'memba that nice, green farmhouse back in Caroliny on Bear Crick Road we used to pass on the way to the sto, and how we would be wishin' and a hopin' that someday it would be ours. Not that we believed it, mind you?"

"Ah do!"

"And how we would picture oursalves in that big ol' house a settin' inside that big ol' winda?"

"Sho do! I 'memba!"

"Ah feels the same way about this place and now it's ours. Can ya'll believe that?"

"Nope! Neva did believe somethin' like this would ever come to us. Nope! Neva did."

Standing by the window, Mr. Richards got their attention. "Lots of luck with the apartment, folks. Oh, I almost forgot. I got you some assistance in the form of a check so you can buy furniture, silverware and pots…you know… towels and things that you'll need. It comes from a fund contributed by our local merchants."

A sudden rush of emotion got the best of Beulah. Bill wiped her eyes with his shirttail. "There you go again, Beulah. I know thems be happy tears, so go on and get her done."

Beulah cocked her head and eyed Richards with a glassy, 'though heartfelt gaze. "Can I give you some sugar, Mista Assemblyman?"

"Of course, Beulah, I've been waiting for that hug all day."

1:15 A.M.
(KNOCK KNOCK KNOCK...BAM!)

Diego threw the blanket to the side and jumped off the couch. **"Who is it?"**

"Police! Open up in there!"

A pair of jeans lay across a chair. "Just a minute!" He hastily put them on, tightened the belt on the way to the door and flicked the light on. He unlatched the bolt lock and eased the door ajar an inch.

On the other side, the Geek reached over Fast Eddie's shoulder and pushed the door open all the way to the wall.

Fast Eddie, said, "Go ahead, move away from da daw...we're comin' in." *(Snap...Pop)* He stepped inside, followed by the Geek who closed the door silently behind him.

Diego was pushed in farther by a hand to his chest.

Fast Eddy said, "So, uh, duz you got a mudder in dat udder room? Go get her, and den sit by dat table, da two o' ya. We got some talkin' to do."

Ana's voice called from the bedroom, troubled and high pitched. "Who is it, Diego?"

"Go ahead, kid, go get her and no funny business," said the Geek.

The Geek made himself comfortable on the couch where he sprawled out with his right leg on top of the cushions as he relit a half smoked cigar. He looked at it and then sucked in a lungful, looked at it again and blew a puff of smoke across the room. He waited quietly while everyone else pulled out chairs and settled in at the table.

Eying Diego and then Ana, he calmly said, "So...where is it?"

Ana, anxious, her hands shaking underneath the table, faced her son who was looking back at her in the same, frightened way. Without hesitation, she ordered him to get the money.

Diego took a deep breath, stood and walked past the Geek. He opened the bottom draw, pushed socks to the side, grabbed the steel box and returned to the table. Placing it in front of Fast Eddie, he took a seat across from him, folded his hands and hung his head.

"Where did you find it?" said the Geek.

Diego looked up and with a quiver in his voice, replied, "In the chimney."

"Damn...how do you like that?"

Removing the gum from his mouth, Fast Eddie stuck it under the seat. "Da chimney! I neva would a taught a dat. How da hell did ya find it dere?"

Searching their surprised faces for even the slightest hint of anger, Diego, said, "One of the stones on top was loose. I was only trying to fix it, but then I saw a rope. I was curious, so, I pulled it up and...well...that's when I saw this grey box."

"Ha! I don't believe it. Wait till I tell Spillane," said the Geek. "He's going to get a kick out of this one."

Fast Eddie glared at Diego. "So...uh...da big sixty four thousand dolla question. Did yas spend any o' da money or is it all in dis box whats here on da table?" He tipped back in his chair and put his hands behind his head to wait for the answer. "Well?"

Diego was more worried than ever.

Do I tell him I spent the 50, or do I let them think Joe did? Is there any way they would know? What if there was more? What if there was $11,000 in that box, 12,000 or even 20,000, and Joe spent the rest of it? They'll think it was me.

More than the huge man that he saw leaning into the couch, the thing that frightened Diego the most was the big, shiny gun fully exposed under his opened jacket. And it wasn't he, himself that he worried about. He worried for his mother.

Fast Eddie, said, "Yeah, you tink about it all you want, kid, we ain't got nowheres else to go at da moment. So make it a good answer. Weez got all night."

"Maybe he does, but I don't," said the Geek. "Come clean, kid. Tell us the truth?"

Diego buried his head under his hands and took another deep breath. He looked upwards at Eddie through the tops of his eyes and forced the words out. "I spent fifty dollars."

(*Sniff Sniff*) Ana wiped her wet cheeks. She knew not to cry out loud. That would certainly anger the two men, but she could only hold in so much, and not for much longer.

"Fifty?"

(Bang)

The side of Eddie's fist slammed down hard on top of the table.

Diego bolted upright.

"Well, guess what? Ya should'na oughta done dat! Dis ain't your money, ya liddle kweep!"

The Geek shouted at Eddie. "Shut up, dummy! Open the box, kid, and let's count it."

Obeying the order, Diego opened it with fumbling fingers.

Eddie quickly snatched the money and spread it across the table in a straight line to make sure the bills were all tens. He then restacked them and broke it all down into hundreds.

"Yep…it's all here, except for da 50 bucks, like da kid said. So let's have it…da 50 or tells us whatever it was dat you taught of in your widdle, kiddy bwain dat you wuz maybe planning on tellin' us…or da coppas, and it better be good."

Fast Eddie continued to glare at Diego, wide eyed for twenty long seconds without an answer coming from the boy.

"Look at dis kid, Big Jimmy. He ain't taught o' nuttin'! Whaddya wanna do?"

"I'm thinking, shut up!"

"Let's bring dems boat back to Spillane."

"I said shut up?"

Eddie grimaced. Addressing Ana, he softly asked, "Say, uh, Mrs. so and so, mind if I use da turly bowl?"

The Geek shook his head. "What the hell are you asking her for? It doesn't matter if you piss on the floor. You're a crook, remember? Who's going to complain? Go use it, so I can think."

The door to the hallway was left wide open as Fast Eddie searched the hallway for the door to the bathroom. He left that one open as well, before going on with his business.

Two inches of Jimmy's cigar was left, and smoking them any further always left an after taste in his mouth. He aimed for the sink and got it in on the first try. He thought to check that his gun was fully loaded, but didn't want to prematurely upset anyone into screaming and waking up the neighbors. Especially, since he wasn't ready to leave yet. His next appointment wasn't for another two and half hours and the ride to the Bronx, at this time of day, took less than one.

"Can I make you some coffee?" Ana meekly asked, her voice barely audible.

"You know what, you read my mind?"

"I apologize, I only have Spanish coffee?"

"As long as it's strong. I'm on the night shift and I got a lot of work to do tonight. I got two in the Bronx and another one in Queens that I still gotta see. What did you spend that money on, kid?"

"I bought my mother a new dress."

"Oh…for her birthday?"

"No…church. She hadn't been to church in a long while. I wanted to do something special for her."

"Yeah, sure, my mother goes to church every Sunday and look what happened to me. So, tell me…were you making plans to spend the rest of this money?"

"I thought I would buy her another dress for a wedding she's supposed to go to on Saturday, but Mom made me promise not to spend another penny of it."

"Is that right, lady?"

Anna responded, cautiously. "I didn't want my son to get into any trouble with this money."

"Well, at least you didn't give it to the cops, because, then, I would've been up shits creek without a paddle. My boss would have had to kiss this money goodbye. How much was the dress?"

Diego looked away. "Around $14.00. I also bought her a pair of shoes."

"You're a good boy to your mother. Especially when the money ain't yours." Jimmy Huffed.

From the bathroom, a prolonged pouring sound, like a horse relieving itself in a galvanized pail, splashed into the bowl. It was followed by a loud flush. Fast Eddie returned and took his place at the table to the smell of coffee brewing.

"So, uh…**what**, are we's all in a diner, now? What's with the making the cawfee, crap?"

The Geek snapped back, "I said it was okay. Leave her alone!"

"We gotta go. What if the coppas are cassin' da joint?"

"They ain't, because Spillane would have known that before he made us come back here. We got eyes and ears in the street, or did you forget?"

Eddie's lips puckered up. "Well, den give me some cawfee. Hey, so what're we doin' with dese two?"

"Nothing!"

"Nuttin'! Waddya talkin' 'bout...**nuttin**'?"

"Just what I said, nothing."

"So, whadabout da fifty? You plannin' to do nuttin' 'bout dat, too?"

"That's right! I'm going to take my time and finish this coffee and then we're taking a ride to the Bronx."

"But da fifty?"

"That's peanuts! We got almost all of the money back and that makes me very happy. And it's also going to make Spillane very happy."

"Jeesh. You're gettin' soft, Big Jimmy."

"What's the point? Can't you see how nice this lady is, and none of it is the kids fault, neither. He found the money. He didn't try to steal it from us like the Barnes did, so what the hell are you mad about?"

"Because!...Dats why! We gotta make an example oudda da boat o' dem."

Ana grabbed Diego's hands and held them in her lap.

The Geek continued, "You see, Eddie, that's why Spillane puts me in charge. You don't think straight. Number one, we got our money. Number two, if anything was to happen to a little boy and his crippled mother in the same building where Barnes lived, there would be a lot more pressure to find out who it was. They already got their eyes on Spillane for what happened to Barnes and Sally Boy. They just can't prove which one of us bumped them off. Well...you know who I mean?"

"Da Barnes? Yeah, dat wuz you!"

"Did you have to mention that in front of these two, you knucklehead?"

"Whud about Tommy? They don't know nuttin' 'bout dat neida!"

"And that was you! Hey, I hope you don't really think they care about Tommy, do you?"

"I don't tink his own mudda cares 'bout him."

"And don't forget about the cop that just fell off this very same roof. This place is very hot right now. There will be a lot more heat on you and me...and Spillane than there is if something else was to happen in this very same building. And no amount of payoffs will keep the cops off our backs. As far as the fifty goes, they can keep it for taking care of our money. They could have skipped town with it. Did you ever think of that?"

Fast Eddie squirmed in his seat and looked the other way. "Mumble, mumble."

"And that takes us to number three, or four, I lost count."

"Which is?"

"That you're an idiot!"

"So I'm an idiot. So shoot me. Oh…shit! Forget I said dat. Hey, we bedda go. We been in dis place too long, already."

"What are you being so jumpy about?"

"Somebody mighta called da coppas."

"Who? Poor people don't have phones."

"Mary, Mary did, and by now dey gotta know who we are."

"So what? We didn't rob the place?"

"What about da Barnes. We wuz in his room? We's was boat in dere, rememba?"

"What does that prove? We had a key."

"An' Mary? You broke her front daw, did ya forget about dat?"

"I didn't forget nothing, Eddie. And who cares? You don't believe she's gonna rat us two out, do you? That was somebody else that broke that door in. Not us! And even if she does snitch on us, who's going to pick us out of a line-up? Not her! If she ever did, she'd be signing her own death warrant, and Spillane would let her know that."

"What about finga prints?"

"Sometimes I wonder why I even let you hang out with me. You're a knucklehead! So what? What the hell does that prove? Barnes was a good friend of ours. We paid him a visit a long time ago, right? In fact, he's the one who introduced us to his girlfriend, fatty Mary. So if they find our finger prints in her room it don't matter, see?"

"Say, do you mind if I go upsteahs right now to see if maybe, uh…you know…if maybe, um, uh…"

"No!"

"Okay!"

"You're also forgetting something else, Eddie. We got ears inside the squad cars. If anything goes down, we're going to know about it first. So, stop fidgeting around and relax. We'll leave when I'm good and ready to leave. In fact, do me a big favor?"

"Whaddya want now?"

"How about you carry that skinny ass of yours out to the car on those pencil legs and wait for me there. You're annoying me."

"Whaddya gonna do to dem."

"You'll see! Just go!"

The Geek stood alongside the couch and stretched. He left his half-filled cup at the edge of the table and followed Eddie to the door. Adjusting his gun, he closed his jacket around it, eased the door shut from the inside, and released the knob gently to silence the clicking sound.

Ana put her arm around Diego with her head on his chest, closed her eyes and silently prayed.

Returning to stand by the table, Jimmy picked up his cup and slowly sipped what was left of the coffee. He put it down and opened his jacket, carelessly knocking the gun to the floor. He glanced at the both of them, huddled together in an embrace before bending down to pick it up. After another glance at Ana, he promptly stuck it back under the waistband.

"I like you two. I don't beat up nice people. I'm letting the both of you go. Like I said before, I got nothing against neither one of you."

Reaching under the Jacket, he repositioned the gun to double check that it was securely in place. Taking out his wallet, he gestured with a slight head nod toward Diego. "Here, kid, take this twenty and buy your mother a nice new dress for that wedding. It's on me."

He followed with another twenty, tossing it on top of the table. "That's for shoes so you can match the dress? And here's twenty more to make up for that dickheaded partner of mine. Have a nice life...and stay out of chimneys."

end

EPILOGUE

Ana borrowed a coat from Karen and went to the wedding with Danny. They eventually married. She got her hip fixed and now lives happily in South Setauket, Long Island. And yes, they dance quite often.

Diego completed college and received a law degree. When time allows, he visits the Jacksons.

Bill and Beulah love the elevator in their building even though they only live on the second floor. It's next door to the Senior Center where Beulah's corn bread and chocolate chip cookies are enjoyed by everyone there. They have a small dog named Chico and are often seen arm in arm strolling the landscaped grounds.

Diego's good friend Larry is with the New York City Transit System, having worked his way up from subway conductor to motorman. He's fat as a whale.

Mary, at the insistence of her sister, Ellen, eventually moved in with her. Ellen is a faithfully committed vegetarian who prides herself in her organic and herb garden. Mary has become devoted to the entirely new life style and is now as thin as Ellen. They both hate Twinkies.

Jerry is a cop in a neighboring precinct and has a family of four. When in the neighborhood, he also checks on the Jacksons.

Leroy teaches High School and coaches baseball.

Jimmy moved to New Jersey, studied business in college and now manages a chain of stores.

Luigi---well, let's call him by his real name, Louis. He owns the building and still lives upstairs. He has a pretty wife and a little girl named Antonia. They vacation every year at Anthony's house in Naples, Italy, where Anthony grows grapes and makes his very own wine.

Now, who do we have left? Oh, yeah, Jose. The D'avino's retired. Jose bought the store and renamed it, "Pier 34 Pet Shop".

Now, I'm sure that step you were sitting on was quite cold when you first sat there, so thanks for listening and giving this old guy a little of your time. Enjoy your walk around the neighborhood. And by the way…if you're a little hungry, try Herzog's around the corner, they have good pizza. Otherwise…**fugedaboudit!**

Dats it

Made in the USA
Charleston, SC
20 August 2015